MALIBU SUMMER

"Jess," Elizabeth said suddenly, "I've changed my mind about Malibu. If you really want to go that badly, I won't hold you back."

The can of soda flew out of Jessica's hand as she dove for her sister, hugging her and shrieking. "Liz, I love you! You're the best sister in the whole world!" she shouted.

"There's only one condition," Elizabeth said, her turquoise eyes serious, "and I really mean it, Jess. You have to take care of all the planning. You have to find the agency and get the jobs and everything. I don't want to end up doing all the work this time. Do you understand?"

Jessica was too ecstatic to let her sister's stern tone upset her. "Don't you worry," she said breathlessly. "I'll do absolutely everything. Just imagine it, we'll both get mother's helper jobs with really rich families—right on the beach! Hollywood-by-the-sea . . . it's the place to spend the summer, Liz. All the stars have places there. We'll both meet fab

the time of our live

Bantam Books in the Sweet Valley High Series
Ask your bookseller for the books you have missed

SWEET VALLEY HIGH
Super Edition

MALIBU SUMMER

Written by
Kate William

Created by
FRANCINE PASCAL

BANTAM BOOKS
TORONTO · NEW YORK · LONDON · SYDNEY · AUCKLAND

RL 6, IL age 12 and up

MALIBU SUMMER
A Bantam Book / August 1986

Sweet Valley High is a trademark of Francine Pascal

Conceived by Francine Pascal

Produced by Cloverdale Press, Inc.

Cover art by James Mathewuse

ISBN 0-553-26050-2

Published simultaneously in the United States and Canada

Bantam Books are published by Bantam Books, Inc. Its trademark, consisting of the
words "Bantam Books" and the portrayal of a rooster, is Registered in U.S. Patent
and Trademark Office and in other countries. Marca Registrada. Bantam Books,
Inc., 666 Fifth Avenue, New York, New York 10103.

PRINTED IN THE UNITED STATES OF AMERICA

O   0 9 8 7 6 5 4 3 2 1

MALIBU SUMMER

One

Elizabeth Wakefield couldn't remember ever feeling so relaxed. She was stretched out on a gigantic striped beach towel, her eyes closed, listening to the magical sound of the waves of the Pacific rolling up on the beach. The strength of the sun and the warm, salty smell of the water were making her sleepier and sleepier, and the best thing of all was knowing that she could doze off if she felt like it. Summer vacation was just beginning, and she didn't have a care in the world!

But the next instant Elizabeth's reverie was shattered. "Here you are!" a familiar voice exclaimed loudly. "Liz, do you realize I've been searching the whole beach for you? You didn't even tell me where you were going to be," Jessica added, injured.

Elizabeth groaned and opened her eyes. "Isn't there some proverb about letting sleeping sisters lie?"

"Not that I know of," Jessica said cheerfully, setting her radio down next to Elizabeth and turning the volume up a notch higher. "I love this song!" She flung her towel and beach bag down enthusiastically and adjusted the antenna on the radio. "Tony Sargent is *so* fantastic!"

"Tony who?" Elizabeth sat up with a sigh, pulling her bathing-suit straps up. It looked as though that nap she had planned was out of the question now.

Jessica's eyes widened in astonishment. She sat back on her heels in dramatic silence. "You can't be serious, Liz," she said finally. "You mean to say you don't know who Tony Sargent is?"

Elizabeth laughed. "Trust me," she said dryly. "I'm ignorant. Who is he?"

Jessica shook her head, her long, blond hair tumbling around her shoulders. "Liz, sometimes I can't even believe you and I are sisters—let alone twins! He's a rock star," she explained, rummaging in her bag. She tossed the magazine onto her sister's towel. "And he's doing a big movie. Isn't he gorgeous?"

Elizabeth glanced down at the cover of the

glossy magazine. The handsome blond boy *did* look familiar, but Elizabeth was enjoying her twin's impatience too much to confess recognition now. It was funny, she thought, rolling over on her stomach and flipping to the story on Tony Sargent's meteoric rise to fame. She and Jessica took for granted the fact that they had completely different interests, just as they took for granted the fact that they were absolutely identical in appearance.

Sixteen years old, the twins had spent their entire lives in the oceanside community of Sweet Valley. Their golden-tanned complexions and soft, sun-streaked hair gave them away as California girls. Even their eyes were California blue, the sparkling, blue-green of the Pacific Ocean. Both were five foot six and slender. When they were younger, they had occasionally dressed alike, especially for family photos or to play silly pranks on their friends. Steven, the twins' eighteen-year-old brother, used to insist they were virtually indistinguishable—until one opened her mouth! When it came to personality, *no one* had any trouble telling which twin was Jessica and which was Elizabeth.

Elizabeth was much more conservative and dependable than Jessica. She worked hard at school and almost always got A's, particularly in her favorite class, English. She dreamed of being a writer one day, and she secretly believed that this ambition had shaped her temperament. Elizabeth always withheld judgment, tried to be a fair observer, and avoided rushing headlong into things. Her writing job for *The Oracle*, Sweet Valley High's school paper, had taught her the value of patience and determination.

Not that Elizabeth's life was all work and no play—far from it! But her idea of fun was usually Jessica's idea of boring. Elizabeth moved more slowly than her hotheaded sister. She loved reading, going to movies, taking long walks—and while she loved being with other people, she preferred small groups to big parties.

Jessica couldn't help being scornful of her sister's idea of fun. Although she adored her twin, Jessica just couldn't help thinking her sister wasted an awful lot of her time—especially by being on the newspaper, for instance. Jessica also thought that Elizabeth's best friend, Enid Rollins, was the biggest wimp imaginable.

Jessica preferred being where the action was. She liked school activities that put her in the spotlight. That was why she was co-captain of the cheerleaders and president of Sweet Valley High's exclusive sorority, Pi Beta Alpha.

Nothing excited Jessica more than *change*. She always wore the newest fashions and listened to the newest music. She didn't like hearing her twin confess she didn't even know who Tony Sargent was. Tony's single, ''You're on My

Mind," had jumped to the top of the charts earlier that month, and Jessica could hardly wait for the release of his movie.

"Speaking of celebrities, Liz," Jessica said slyly, rubbing some oil on her tanned calves, "have you given any more thought to what I said last night about Malibu?"

Elizabeth laughed. "I wondered how long it would be before you started working on me again!" she replied. "I told you, Jess, I really have my heart set on getting an internship with the *Sweet Valley News* this summer. It would be so good for me to get a chance to work at a real paper, especially if—"

"Liz," Jessica said, pouting, "you *know* Mom and Dad said they wouldn't let me get a job in Malibu by myself! I'm going to die if I have to stay here this summer." She peered at her twin, who was not reacting to her anguish. "Liz, just imagine it," she said excitedly, trying another tack. "We could both get mother's helper jobs with really rich families, right on the beach! Hollywood by the sea—it's *the* place to spend the summer. All the stars have places there. We'll both meet fabulous guys. We'll have the time of our lives! And," she added pointedly, "we'll be on our own."

Frowning, Elizabeth slipped her sunglasses out of her bag and put them on. "I think you're making the job sound a lot more glamorous than it really is, Jessica. What makes you think the families will be really rich? Or that we wouldn't have to work really hard, taking care of the kids?"

Jessica shrugged. "Because Lila says—" She clapped her hand over her mouth and turned bright red.

Elizabeth's eyes narrowed. "Aha!" she said, nodding her head in sudden comprehension. "I knew there had to be a catch! What does Lila have to do with all this?"

Lila Fowler and Jessica had been friends for years, but their relationship suffered so many ups and downs that Elizabeth didn't even know whether "friendship" was the best term for it. They were fiercely competitive about everything from clothes to boyfriends, and in general it was safe to say that if Lila had something, Jessica would want it—and vice versa.

Unfortunately for Jessica, Lila was the only child of one of the richest men in Sweet Valley. Mr. Fowler's computer business had made him a millionaire practically overnight, and he loved reminding people of how much he was worth. All Lila had to do was point at something, and it was hers. Jessica knew she couldn't compete with Lila financially, but there was a lot more to life than just plain money, and Jessica knew she was well-equipped to compete with Lila when it came to everything else!

Jessica glanced casually around the beach. She knew Elizabeth thought Lila was petty and spoiled. She had deliberately tried to keep Lila's job a secret until she had persuaded Elizabeth to change her mind. Now she was going to have to try a new approach. "Lila's dad got her a job in Malibu," Jessica admitted.

Elizabeth looked surprised. "Lila? Working? Isn't that kind of unusual?"

Jessica smiled. "You're not kidding! Lila's never worked a day in her life. Supposedly Mr. Fowler thinks she needs some work experience. He thinks it'll help her build character."

Elizabeth giggled. "I can't imagine Lila changing diapers all summer."

"Oh, don't worry about that," Jessica said. "Mr. Fowler has some big client whose son's got a place in Malibu. The son is married, and they have one two-year-old and a nanny, and about three other people to take care of him. Lila's just supposed to play with him sometimes and read him stories at night. It doesn't sound too taxing.'"

Elizabeth looked thoughtful. "And you want to get a job in Malibu so you can be with Lila for the summer?"

Jessica looked pained. "Not really. Honestly, Liz, Lila has nothing to do with it. I just think it sounds unbelievably good, that's all. And," she added, lowering her eyes, "I just want to share the best summer in the world with my favorite twin."

Elizabeth rolled her eyes. "If Mom and Dad hadn't said you could only go if I did, something tells me you'd be more than willing to leave 'your favorite twin'!"

"Shh," Jessica said, looking quickly over her shoulder. "There's Lila now. Let's wait and talk more about it later, OK?"

Elizabeth shrugged. "Whatever you say."

Jessica had already told Lila what her parents had said, and Lila had promised to help Jessica work on her sister. Lila wanted Jessica to come to Malibu almost as much as Jessica wanted it herself, and Lila was used to getting her way.

"You two are both so tanned already," Lila complained in greeting. She slithered out of her sun dress, revealing a leather-look maillot that Elizabeth privately thought far too mature for her. "What do you think?" Lila asked, pivoting so they could see the deep vee in back. "Will this be a hit in Malibu, or what?"

Elizabeth laughed. "I'm sure it'll stand out."

Jessica's eyes shone. "It's perfect, Li," she pronounced. She winked at her friend, patting her towel invitingly. "I was just telling Liz what a wonderful summer you're going to have."

"Wonderful," Lila said dramatically, "is *not* the word. This summer is going to be the most important, the most—the most significant—"

"I told you she was excited." Jessica giggled.

"I am more than excited," Lila said. "I've already decided I'm going to fall madly in love this summer."

"With whom?" Elizabeth asked, amused.

Lila gave her a scathing look. "Who knows?" she said airily, waving her hand. "There are a lot of great-looking girls in Malibu."

"So?" Elizabeth said, laughing.

Jessica sent Lila a defeated glance. "It's no use," she said sadly. "Liz doesn't realize how great Malibu is going to be, Lila."

Lila frowned and turned back to Elizabeth. "You can't tell me you'd rather spend the summer hanging around *here*." She made it sound as if that was the worst thing in the whole world.

"I wouldn't mind. I was thinking of getting an internship with the *News*," Elizabeth said cheerfully.

Lila looked horrified. "The *News*? You mean you'd really spend your whole summer *inside*?"

"Forget it," Jessica said gloomily. "She won't listen, Lila. I've already tried."

"What kind of men are you planning on meeting at the *News*?" Lila added, her brown eyes widening as it occurred to her just how dire the situation really was.

Elizabeth shook her head. "I don't want to work there to meet men. I want to learn to be a better writer!"

9

"This is serious," Lila said to Jessica.

"You're telling me," Jessica said. The next minute she was on her feet, poking through her coin purse. "Does anyone want anything? I'm going up to the snack bar for a soda."

"No, thanks," Elizabeth said, unearthing her novel and opening it to the bookmark.

"This probably isn't any of my business," Lila said when Jessica was out of earshot, "but don't you think you're being kind of selfish, Liz?"

Elizabeth stared at her. "What do you mean?"

"Just that Jessica has her heart set on going to Malibu, that's all. And your parents won't let her go unless you go, too. Don't you think you could forget about the *News* for Jessica's sake?"

Elizabeth put down her book. "You really think Jessica wants to go that badly?" she asked, her mouth dry. The last thing Elizabeth wanted to do was hurt her sister. She had assumed the mother's helper job was just another one of her sister's whims, but if Jessica really had her heart set on it and Elizabeth was all that stood in her way . . .

"I know she does," Lila asserted, snapping open a compact mirror and examining the bridge of her nose for freckles. "Believe me, Liz, if she doesn't get to go, she'll probably do something desperate!"

Elizabeth didn't say anything for a minute. "If it really matters that much to her . . ." she murmured. She didn't notice Lila's triumphant smile. She was reshuffling her plans in her mind, wondering if she could arrange an internship for after school in the fall or the following summer.

Jessica was walking toward them, a can of cold soda in her hand.

"Jess," Elizabeth said suddenly, "I've changed my mind about Malibu. If you really want to go *that* badly, I won't hold you back."

The can of soda flew out of Jessica's hand as she dove for her sister, hugging her and shrieking. "Liz, I love you! You're the best sister in the whole world!" she shouted, kicking sand all over Lila in her enthusiasm.

"Hey, cut it out!" Lila exclaimed.

"There's only one condition," Elizabeth said, her turquoise eyes serious, "and I really mean it, Jess. You have to take care of all the planning. *You* have to find the agency and get the jobs and everything. I'll go with you when it's time to interview, but that's it. I don't want to end up doing all the work this time. Do you understand?"

Jessica was too ecstatic to let her sister's stern tone upset her. "Don't you worry," she said breathlessly. "I'll do absolutely everything." She giggled. "I've already got an appointment with Mrs. Norman at Nannies and Company this afternoon!"

Elizabeth groaned. "You really thought you

could change my mind all along," she accused her twin.

"Liz, thank you so much," Jessica said passionately. "I promise you, you won't regret this!"

As Elizabeth regarded her twin, she had a sinking feeling in the pit of her stomach. The truth was, she was beginning to regret it already.

Who knew what kind of summer she was in for now?

Two

Jessica parked the red convertible Fiat she shared with her sister in front of the small brick building, then checked her reflection in the rearview mirror. She knew how important this interview was. Mrs. Norman, the director of Nannies and Company, was choosy about the girls she took on. Her agency served some of the most exclusive families in Southern California, and she made sure the girls who worked for her were the best. Jessica was wearing an uncharacteristically conservative outfit for the appointment, a striped, button-down shirt and matching blue skirt, borrowed from Elizabeth. She just *had* to make a good impression, she thought. Now that she had convinced Elizabeth to come with her to

Malibu, Mrs. Norman was all that was standing between Jessica and her dream summer!

Ten minutes later she was perched nervously on the edge of a chair in Mrs. Norman's plush office. "Miss Wakefield?" the director said inquiringly, opening a manila file. Patricia Norman was in her early fifties, but with her stylishly short, steel-gray hair and slim, elegant figure, she was still extremely attractive. Jessica sneaked appreciative glances around the office. Signed photos of Mrs. Norman posing with celebrities decorated the walls. Maybe a celebrity's family needed a mother's helper this summer!

Jessica could barely contain her enthusiasm. Within minutes she had told Patricia Norman all about herself and Elizabeth. "We're hoping to find jobs that aren't too far apart," she concluded eagerly. "We were thinking of Malibu, in fact."

Mrs. Norman smiled. "You and your sister are twins, you say?" She adjusted her glasses, looking thoughtful. "I like that." She nodded her head seriously. "We don't have any twins working for Nannies and Company. I have a feeling some of our clients might really like the idea. Tell me what kind of work experience you've had, dear."

Jessica thought quickly. "I've had quite a bit," she said. Remembering that Lila had said babies were preferable to toddlers because all they did was sleep, she added, "I'm especially experienced with infants."

"Good," Mrs. Norman said. "As a matter of fact, we *do* still have a few jobs available for the summer in Malibu, but only one family is looking for someone to take care of an infant."

"That sounds perfect," Jessica said, delighted. Suddenly remembering Elizabeth, she added, "Only one?" A pang of guilt struck her, but the next instant she convinced herself that Elizabeth liked challenges. Elizabeth would probably be delighted to be in charge of an older child.

"Yes—the Sargents." Mrs. Norman flipped through the file. "They're quite young, and they have just one child, a boy, Sam."

"The Sargents," Jessica repeated, her brow furrowing. "They're not related to Tony Sargent, are they?"

Mrs. Norman smiled. "I believe they're cousins," she said. "That doesn't bother you, does it?"

Jessica's eyes flashed. "No!" Her voice was high with excitement. "I mean, no, that's fine," she added hastily, trying to contain herself. She couldn't believe her luck. It was a dream come true! She'd be living with Tony Sargent's cousin that summer, taking care of a perfect little baby. Tony would probably drop by practically all the time. Within days he and Jessica would be fast friends, and then . . .

"Now," Mrs. Norman was saying, "the only other job we have available in Malibu is with the Bennets, Malcolm and Audrey." She frowned. "They're nice people, but I'm a little reluctant. . . . Is your sister very good with children? I'm afraid their little girl is kind of a handful."

Jessica forced Tony Sargent out of her mind for the moment. "Liz is wonderful with kids," she said earnestly. "Especially with problem kids. She really loves challenges." She brushed aside her second pang of guilt. Elizabeth wouldn't mind, she told herself. The little girl couldn't be *that* bad!

"Well," Mrs. Norman said and sighed, "we had some complaints from the girl who took care of Taryn last year. Apparently she's fairly difficult, but she may have changed. If you're sure your sister can handle her . . ."

"I'm positive," Jessica said firmly. "Honestly, Mrs. Norman. You should see Liz. She's so good at everything! I bet she'll have Taryn wrapped around her little finger by the end of the summer."

"Here's your information card on the Sargents, dear." Mrs. Norman still looked doubtful. "And here's the card on the Bennets. Of course, I'll need to meet your sister. Have her drop by as soon as she can. Once we're all set, I'd like you girls to call and arrange interviews with the clients. They'll want to meet you sometime this weekend. As long as everything goes without a hitch, they'll call and confirm with us, and you've got the jobs. How does that sound to you?"

"That's fine," Jessica said, tucking the precious cards in her handbag.

She felt as though she were practically floating as Mrs. Norman showed her out of the office.

Tony Sargent! She still couldn't believe her luck. Just wait until Lila heard about *this*!

Practically overnight Tony Sargent had turned into the biggest sensation in years. He was only seventeen, and he already had two gold records and a contract for his first movie. To Jessica, the amazing thing about Tony, though, was how natural he seemed. Every time she saw him in a magazine she was struck by the frank, almost innocent expression in his wide blue eyes. With his streaked blond hair and gorgeous tan, he looked more like a surfer than a celebrity. And his voice! "You're on My Mind" made shivers run up and down Jessica's back. When he sang the lines "But, baby, still I find/ That you're on my mind," Jessica felt like crying. His voice really got to her. It sounded rough and scratchy and incredibly loving and sexy all at the same time.

Tony Sargent might not know she was alive yet, but he would! Jessica barely noticed the scenery around her as she drove home. She was picturing a Malibu sunset, with the waves crashing up on the beach as she and Tony walked hand in hand along the shore . . .

It was like a dream come true, getting an interview at the Sargents'. Jessica could hardly wait until everything was confirmed and she and Elizabeth were certain they had the jobs!

"Liz, you're not going to believe how wonderful this summer's going to be!" Jessica said excitedly, bursting into her sister's bedroom.

Elizabeth looked up from her journal and shook her head. "Something tells me I'm about to be convinced."

"Mrs. Norman loved the idea of having twins work for Nannies and Company," she said as she bounced onto Elizabeth's bed. "And she's got two jobs in Malibu, Liz! They both sound *so* good."

Elizabeth wrote one last word and closed her journal. "You mean there really are two jobs in Malibu?" She was surprised.

Jessica chuckled happily. "You didn't think it was going to work out so easily, did you? But, Liz, it's all so simple! We just have to call the people and set up interviews for this weekend. And that's it! We drive up to Malibu, make some small talk, and the jobs are ours! Oh—and one

18

more thing. You need to meet with Mrs. Norman," she added quickly. "But it's just a formality."

"It sounds easy enough," Elizabeth agreed thoughtfully. "What are the families like? Did you find out anything about the kids?"

Jessica thought quickly. There didn't seem to be any point mentioning Tony Sargent. After all, Elizabeth hadn't even heard of him before that morning. What difference would it make to her that he just happened to be related to the family Jessica had staked out as *hers*?

Nor could it do any good to worry Elizabeth in advance about Taryn Bennet. Better let her twin go up to Malibu with an open mind!

"Well," Jessica said, the truth quickly dissolving in her eagerness to keep Elizabeth on her side, "*your* job sounds really easy. It's just one little girl who's already old enough to take care of herself."

"How old?" Elizabeth asked skeptically.

"Six or seven." Jessica waved a hand vaguely. "Here's the information card. Just call Mrs. Bennet and set up a time to see her."

"What's *your* family like?" Elizabeth eyed her twin suspiciously.

Jessica blinked. "Uh—well, I thought *I'd* take the job that sounds like more work, since you're being so sweet to come with me," she fibbed.

19

Elizabeth raised her eyebrows. "Why? What's with your family?"

"Oh, they have a little baby boy," Jessica said quickly. "Mrs. Norman said he's quite a handful, but I don't mind—honestly, Liz. All I care about is getting to spend the summer in Malibu—and having you really close by!"

Elizabeth looked at the card Jessica had handed her. "Well, that's awfully nice of you," she said slowly. "But are you sure, Jess? I'd be happy to take the baby if you think he's going to be so hard to look after."

"No!" Jessica was horrified. "I mean, that's really sweet of you, Liz, but I think *I* should have the harder job. It's only fair."

Elizabeth shrugged. "OK, if that's what you really want."

"So, as soon as you talk to Mrs. Norman, we should call and set up appointments for Saturday afternoon. Then we'll just drive up in the morning, have lunch, and—" Jessica's face suddenly drained of color. "Omigosh!" she shrieked, clapping her hand over her mouth.

"What is it?" Elizabeth demanded anxiously. "What's wrong? You look like you just saw a ghost!"

"I just remembered! I have to go to cheerleading camp this weekend. We're leaving Friday for Timber Falls."

Elizabeth stared at her. "Can't you get out of it?"

Jessica shook her head, crushed. "I'm the co-captain," she reminded her sister. "Robin and I are supposed to lead all sorts of special sessions on routines, cheering, pep rallies. There's no way I can get out of it! Liz, our whole summer's ruined!"

Jessica's face had crumpled with disappointment. "Maybe we could go up to Malibu next weekend," Elizabeth said hopefully, putting a consoling hand on her twin's arm.

Jessica shook her head. "Mrs. Norman said we have to take care of it this weekend. Otherwise, she'll give our spots away to some other girls. Oh, Liz, I can't believe it." She seemed to be close to tears. "Of all the lousy luck . . ."

"It *is* bad luck," Elizabeth agreed. "But it doesn't seem like there's anything we can do about it."

"Well, there *is* something." Jessica's eyes had brightened a little, and now she was gazing intently at her sister.

"I can't think what," Elizabeth said, picking up her journal again. "Jess, quit *looking* at me that way!"

"Liz," Jessica wheedled, "couldn't you—just this once—go up to Malibu on Saturday and interview for both of us?"

"No," Elizabeth said firmly. "I couldn't."

"Why?" Jessica wailed, anguished. "Liz, it's the only way! You can't say no!"

"I can and I am," Elizabeth said, pretending to look for an entry in her journal. "It's out of the question, Jess."

"Oh, come on," Jessica begged. "*Please*, Liz. It wouldn't be that much trouble! All you have to do is—"

"Look," Elizabeth said, turning to face her sister. "You know I'm not that big on the idea in the first place, and you said you'd take care of everything. Remember? I refuse to end up doing all the work this summer while you have a great time. And that's all there is to it!"

Jessica was quiet for a minute, her lower lip quivering. "Well, OK," she whispered finally. A tear slid down one smooth, tanned cheek. "I didn't want to go *that* badly. Something else will turn up for the summer."

Elizabeth didn't say anything, but Jessica could tell she was weakening.

"Thanks anyway, Liz," she said softly. "You've been great about it. I'm not kidding."

"I can't stand it!" Elizabeth exclaimed, throwing her journal against the wall with a bang. "I give in. But *you* have to call and set up the appointments. And you'd better make sure you leave me enough time to get from one place to the other!"

"Liz, you're the best sister in the whole world!"

"What are their names, anyway?" Elizabeth asked.

"Yours are named Bennet," Jessica said.

"I know that. It's on the card," Elizabeth said. "I meant *yours*."

"Oh . . . I think it's Sargent," Jessica said offhandedly.

"Sargent? Like Tony Sargent—the singer you were talking about?"

Jessica turned pink. Leave it to Elizabeth to have a good memory at a time like this. "Yeah," she said hastily. "But it's just a coincidence. It's really a common name."

She couldn't see what good it would do to let Elizabeth know that Tony was the Sargents' cousin. It was risky enough letting Elizabeth go up to Malibu alone that weekend! Jessica had no idea how her sister would react when she saw the discrepancy between sweet little Sam and terrible Taryn.

At this point all she could do was cross her fingers and wait.

Three

"Wow," Elizabeth breathed, staring in amazement at the spectacular white house in front of her. She checked the directions on the seat beside her again, certain she'd made a mistake. But this was it. 400 Ocean Avenue. The Bennets' house. In Elizabeth's brief appointment at the agency, Mrs. Norman had given her no hint that the Bennets lived in a place this magnificent.

Elizabeth pulled the Fiat up the steep driveway. Though Malibu wasn't more than an hour and a half from Sweet Valley, Elizabeth had never been there, and she had to admit it was every bit as gorgeous as Jessica had promised. The spectacular, ruddy Southern California mountains dropped sharply to the ocean, and above the sparkling white beaches, dozens of wonderful beach houses seemed to be carved out of the cliffs.

The Bennets had one of the most beautiful houses on this exclusive strip. Elizabeth had never seen a place like this, except in the movies. The house was enormous. With its white stucco facade glittering in the sunlight and sparkling red-tile roof, it looked like a Mediterranean villa.

Elizabeth parked the car behind a spotless white Jaguar and took a deep breath. The house was right on the beach; the diamond-blue Pacific sparkled before her. *Imagine having the beach right in your own backyard!* she thought. She walked up to the front door and hesitated, then pressed the bell. The door opened, and a woman of Mexican descent looked inquiringly at her.

"I'm Elizabeth Wakefield," Elizabeth said pleasantly. "I have an appointment with Mrs. Bennet. I'm interviewing to be a mother's helper this summer."

"Ah!" The woman threw up her hands. "Come in, come in," she urged warmly. "I'm afraid Mrs. Bennet isn't home. I think she may have forgotten your appointment."

"But I drove all the way from Sweet Valley," Elizabeth said, crestfallen. "How could she—I mean, how—"

"Don't worry." The woman smiled. "Come in," she repeated, leading Elizabeth through a long hallway into an enormous, cathedral-ceilinged room looking out over the ocean. "I'm Maria. I work for the Bennets," she said in a slightly accented voice, "and they are very, very busy. But it doesn't matter. I can interview you for Mrs. Bennet. I spend a great deal of time with Taryn."

Elizabeth was mystified. She sank down into the white leather chair to which Maria pointed. She couldn't imagine what would keep Mrs. Bennet from being here to interview her. What could be more important than her little girl's welfare?

But Maria quickly put her at ease. She was in her twenties, and her warmth and lively sense of humor helped Elizabeth to relax. In no time she and Maria were trading anecdotes about Sweet Valley. Maria's cousin worked there, and she had visited the town several times.

"You seem ideal for the job," Maria said finally, smiling at Elizabeth. "But I should say . . ." She frowned and looked away. "This is a strange household. An unhappy household, perhaps. Mrs. Bennet goes out all the time, too. You'll find yourself alone with Taryn most of the time."

Elizabeth swallowed. She couldn't help feeling uneasy. "Can I meet Taryn? I'd like a chance to say hello to her."

"Of course! She's up in her room. I'll give you a tour of the house, and you can meet her then."

Maria looked closely at Elizabeth. "I don't want to put you off the job because you seem like such a nice girl and I'm sure you'll be wonderful. But Taryn can be a bit difficult at first. She's very shy. She's had a lonely life, and sometimes. . . ." Her voice trailed off.

What a strange place! Elizabeth thought. It was odd for Mrs. Bennet to leave her little girl alone all the time. It really sounded as if the Bennets didn't have much of a family life, or much of a marriage either, for that matter.

"Come." Maria stood up and smiled. "Let me give you a quick tour."

For the next twenty minutes Elizabeth followed Maria from room to room. The house was extraordinary. The ceilings were high, and enormous windows opened out on breathtaking views of the Pacific. The design of the house and the furniture were very modern. Liz thought of her mother, an interior designer, and of how much she would enjoy touring this mansion. The house was built around a central courtyard, with a swimming pool and a complete outdoor bar. There was a tennis court and an indoor gym.

It was a beautiful house, but something about it seemed cold to Elizabeth. She couldn't imagine being a little girl in that house. Where did Taryn play?

"And this," Maria said, throwing open a door beyond which ran a long corridor, "is Taryn's wing." Elizabeth's eyes widened as they passed a playroom and a TV room, finally reaching a huge bedroom filled with toys and dolls of every size and description. In the corner a little girl was forlornly pushing a doll in a baby carriage.

"Taryn," Maria said gently, "I want you to meet someone."

"I don't want to," Taryn said sullenly, looking away.

Elizabeth gave Maria a quick, questioning look. Maria nodded. "Hi, Taryn," Elizabeth said, crossing the room to kneel by the child's side. "What's your doll's name?"

Taryn glared. "She doesn't have a name," she said, grabbing the doll out of the carriage.

Elizabeth took a deep breath. "Well, *my* name is Elizabeth," she said cheerfully. "I'm going to stay with you this summer. I'm going to help take care of you."

"I don't need anyone to take care of me," Taryn retorted, her large, violet-blue eyes filling with tears. "Go 'way. My doll and me want to be alone, please."

"Did I say something wrong?" Elizabeth whispered to Maria as they left the room together.

Maria shook her head. "No, that's just the way she is." Her brown eyes fixed seriously on Elizabeth's. "Do you think you'd like the job, even now that you've met Taryn? Some applicants have turned it down."

Elizabeth swallowed. "Yes," she said finally. "I would—as long as you think I'm capable of handling her."

Maria sighed. "She's had a lonely life, poor thing, but, yes, I think you could do her a world of good. I'll tell Mrs. Bennet that I think you're an ideal candidate for the job."

Elizabeth wasn't quite certain what to say. Her heart ached for Taryn, but she couldn't help feeling apprehensive. She knew she would like to help the little girl. It wasn't going to be easy, but she was more than willing to try.

Half an hour later Elizabeth pulled the Fiat up in front of a small ranch house several blocks from the beach. She shook her head, smiling. "Jess wasn't kidding," she said aloud. "She really *did* give me a break." The Sargent house was ordinary by any standard, and compared to the Bennet place it was postage-stamp size! Elizabeth felt like giggling as she walked up the front path. Then she remembered she was masquerading as Jessica; she had to be on her best behavior to make sure her sister got the job.

Elizabeth needn't have worried. Lucy and John Sargent were two of the nicest, most easygoing people she'd ever met. She was in her late twenties, and he was about thirty, but they both seemed years younger. Lucy had red hair and was wearing jeans and a UCLA T-shirt, and Josh was wearing track shorts. They both kept tripping over each other. "This place is too small!" Lucy said, pretending to tear her hair out.

She was right—it *was* small. The master bedroom was filled with boxes—books, they explained, that they didn't have room to unpack. The baby's room was tiny. A cot had been squeezed into it, amidst Sam's furniture.

"I hope you don't mind sharing a room with Sam," Lucy said, smiling down at the baby in her arms. "We *do* have a little guest room, but it's filled with junk right now. And anyway, it's off the porch. You wouldn't be able to hear Sammy if he cried."

"No," Elizabeth said, suppressing a smile as she looked at the crowded nursery. "This is fine!" She wondered where Jessica was going to put all her clothes, not to mention her makeup and jewelry. It was going to be a tight squeeze.

But she couldn't help admiring the natural affection Lucy and Josh showed each other and their newborn son. What this family may have lacked in glamour they made up for in genuine warmth. Lucy insisted on getting Elizabeth a glass of iced tea. While she was preparing a tray in the kitchen, Elizabeth held Sam on her lap and talked with Josh, who turned out to be a freelance writer. "Really?" Elizabeth exclaimed eagerly. "I'm really—I mean, my sister Elizabeth is really interested in writing," she corrected herself hastily. "Maybe she can come over sometime this summer and talk to you about your career."

"Sure," boomed Josh, coming over to tickle Sam. When Lucy returned, the two outlined the responsibilities they envisioned for Jessica that summer. It sounded like a lot of work to Elizabeth. They really needed help, that much was clear. Lucy was an artist, and she planned to take some classes. They were going to get their money's worth out of Jessica.

No doubt about it, Elizabeth thought, Jessica was being incredibly generous. Living with the Sargents might be more *fun* than living with the Bennets, but it also looked as though it was going to be exhausting!

She felt more than a little surprised that Jessica was really willing to let her live in splendor, in her own private wing of the Bennet mansion, while Jessica slaved, changing diapers in a tiny house blocks from the sea.

It's just another sign that I've misjudged her, Elizabeth told herself. *Jessica is obviously more generous than I've given her credit for*.

She could hardly wait to get home to tell her sister that they'd done it. They both had jobs wrapped up for what was beginning to look like an interesting summer!

Four

"I don't know how I'm going to stand it around here without you this summer," Enid Rollins said, her green eyes grave as she watched Elizabeth walk from her closet to the open suitcase on her bed and back to her dresser again.

"I'm going to miss you, too," Elizabeth told her sincerely. She shook her head, her blond ponytail bobbing. "I honestly don't even know how Jessica managed to rope me into this whole thing!"

"You promise to write? I want to know absolutely everything!"

Elizabeth smiled. "I promise," she said. "And you have to keep me informed, too! Malibu isn't that far away. We'll be able to talk on the phone.

And maybe you can visit. My parents will be up on the Fourth of July. You could come with them!"

Enid shook her head. "I doubt it, Liz. Not if I'm really going to get a job like I promised my mom."

Elizabeth frowned at the bikini in her hand. "I wonder how much spare time I'll have," she murmured. "You know, Enid, Taryn really seems like a strange little girl to me. I hope I can handle her."

"If anyone can, you can, Liz," Enid said loyally.

Just then her bedroom door burst open, and Jessica stuck her head inside. "Liz, aren't you ready yet?" she wailed. "I've been downstairs for ages!"

"I'm almost ready," Elizabeth assured her. A teasing smile crossed her face. "I hope you didn't pack much, Jess. Remember how small the Sargents' house is."

Jessica gave her a dirty look. "It can't be *that* small," she said crossly. "Listen, I'll be downstairs. Hurry up!"

"What was all that about?" asked Enid.

Elizabeth giggled. "Jessica refuses to believe the house she's working at is really tiny! She thinks I'm making it up just to bug her."

Enid laughed. "I wish I could be there to see

her face when she opens the front door. Didn't you say she'd be sleeping in the baby's room?"

Elizabeth nodded as she slipped a makeup kit and hairbrush into her suitcase, then zipped it up. "That ought to do it. I guess I'd better go down and say goodbye to my parents and Steve. Jessica's probably about to take off without me."

"What are you two going to do about sharing the car this summer?" Enid took one of Elizabeth's bags and followed her down the stairs.

"I think I'll let Jessica keep it at the Sargents'." She giggled. "Among other things, she doesn't believe their house is six *long* blocks from the beach. Something tells me she's going to want the car when she finds out I wasn't kidding. Besides, the Bennets seem to have cars to spare."

"It's about time," Jessica said when she saw Elizabeth. "I promised Lila we'd call her at the Jonsons' as soon as we got to Malibu and go out for a hamburger in town." Jessica scowled. Lila had left a few days before the twins. "But if we don't get going soon, we'll be meeting her for breakfast tomorrow instead!"

"OK, OK," Elizabeth said, smiling at her sister. She opened the front door and took her bags out to the Fiat. "Where're Mom and Dad? And Steve?" she called back over her shoulder.

"They're out back on the patio. Should I tell them we're leaving?"

"Sure," Elizabeth said, laughing. To Enid she

added in a whisper, "I haven't seen Jessica this eager to get anywhere in my entire life!"

A minute later Mr. and Mrs. Wakefield were also standing in the driveway, showering the girls with last-minute suggestions and concerns. "You're sure you checked the tires, honey?" Mr. Wakefield asked, anxiously inspecting the Fiat.

"Yes, Daddy." Jessica tapped her foot impatiently.

Elizabeth gave her father a quick hug. Dark-haired and athletic, he was an older version of the twins' brother Steven, who had trailed his parents out to say goodbye. "I'm going to miss you two clones," Steven said, rumpling the twins' hair. "What am I going to do for aggravation around here this summer with you guys so far away?"

"I'm sure you'll find a substitute," Jessica said, giggling.

"You both promise to call tonight to let us know you've arrived safely?" Mrs. Wakefield asked, pushing her blond hair back from her face. Elizabeth felt a sudden rush of love as she looked at her mother's smooth, unlined face and gentle blue eyes. She realized then that she was going to miss her family very much that summer. They would see their parents on the Fourth of July, but suddenly that seemed a long way off. Apparently Jessica had the same feeling. The next thing anyone knew she was throwing her arms around first her father, then her mother, then Steven.

"What gives?" Steven growled, pretending to shake her loose. Then he pulled her back into a big bear hug. "If any of those Malibu men give you a hard time, you know who to call."

"Yeah, but who should she call if they don't give her a hard time?" Elizabeth winked at Enid. Jessica pretended to take a swipe at her, and they all laughed.

At last the twins were bundled into the Fiat. "Don't forget to water my plants!" Elizabeth called to Steven as Jessica turned the key in the ignition. Waving goodbye, the twins pulled out of the driveway. They were off at last, and from Jessica's immense sigh of relief, Elizabeth had a feeling their Malibu summer was getting started not a minute too soon!

"You really didn't believe me, did you?" Elizabeth asked. They were parked in front of the Bennets', and Jessica was staring, open-mouthed, at the huge beachside palace.

"This place is just incredible." She shook her head in amazement. "I can't believe it!"

"Well, I told you," Elizabeth reminded her. A sudden thought crossed her mind. If Jessica really hadn't known about the differences between the Bennets and the Sargents, she couldn't have purposely given Elizabeth the "better" job. Maybe Elizabeth had given Jessica too much credit; it was starting to look as though she'd gotten the cushier situation merely by chance.

Jessica swallowed. She tried to sound cheerful as she said, "Of course, Mrs. Norman *told* me the Bennets had a spectacular house. I just thought *you* should get to work here, since you were so nice about coming to Malibu."

Elizabeth took her suitcases out of the car. "Well, thanks for the ride." She shook her head as she faced the enormous house. "This sure feels weird," she admitted. "What time are you picking me up for dinner, Jess? Did you and Lila set a time?"

"Six-thirty." Jessica sat in a daze, her hands loose on the steering wheel. "Do you have the Sargents' number in case you need to get in touch with me?"

"Yes." Elizabeth hoisted a bag in each hand, flashing her twin an ironic smile. "I *was* there, pretending to be you, remember?"

"Well, see you soon." Jessica watched her sister head up the brick walk to the front door, where she was met by a dark-haired woman. Elizabeth and her belongings disappeared inside. Jessica pulled the Fiat away from the curb.

She couldn't believe the Bennets' house. What

a place! So Elizabeth hadn't been telling her all that stuff about an indoor gym and courtyard and suites just to bug her—which meant that the Sargents' place really might be as small as she'd said, too.

Jessica's heart sank. It had never even occurred to her to ask Mrs. Norman where the two houses were located or how big they were. From what Lila had intimated, Jessica had just assumed that everyone in Malibu had a mansion right on the ocean. Lila's place was apparently nice enough, and Elizabeth's . . .

Jessica pulled the Fiat up to the address listed on the agency card. Her worse fears were confirmed. "This can't be it," she whispered, staring in dismay at the tiny ranch house. It was so *small*!

Taking a deep and—she imagined—noble breath, Jessica got out of the Fiat, slinging one of her bags over her shoulder. Elizabeth hadn't been kidding when she warned her not to bring too much stuff. If only she had listened! She had four suitcases with her, and from the looks of the house, she would be lucky to find room for a handbag.

Jessica gritted her teeth as she marched up the front walk. She stabbed the door bell once, shifting her bag from one shoulder to the next, and stabbed it again just as the door opened and a young man in jeans and a cut-off sweatshirt grinned out at her.

"Jessica!" he cried. "Come on in!"

Jessica blinked. She had forgotten that she had supposedly already met the Sargents. "Uh—hi, Josh," she said, hoping she'd gotten his name right.

"Lucy's changing Sam," Josh told her, taking her bag. "Is this all you brought?"

"No . . . actually, I have a few more bags," Jessica said, peering miserably into the cluttered front hallway.

"I'll put this in Sam's room. Why don't you sit down and relax while I get the rest of your stuff?"

Before Jessica could answer, Lucy emerged from a small room off the hallway, a freshly diapered Sam in her arms. "Hi, Jess!" She reached out to shake Jessica's hand. The telephone rang, and Lucy shifted the baby and looked about her. "Where's Josh?"

"He's outside getting my bags," Jessica said, staring at Sam. He was so tiny! She hadn't realized a three-month-old baby would be that small.

"Here, Jess. Will you hold Sam while I get the phone?" Lucy passed the squirming bundle to Jessica, who gulped and hugged him to her awkwardly.

"Hi, Sammy," she offered halfheartedly. Sam

40

kicked one miniature leg as hard as he could, hitting her in mid-chest. Jessica winced. The next minute he let out an incredible scream, his little face screwing up as if he were in pain. Jessica stood helplessly rooted to the spot.

"You've got an awful lot of stuff," Josh called, staggering in under the rest of her luggage. "I'm not sure we're going to have space for you in Sam's room once we get all this in there!"

Jessica felt depressed. Sam was still wailing, and all she could think to do was to hold him to her chest and pat him awkwardly on his tiny back. "Stop that," she whispered desperately.

Jessica couldn't believe she really had to share a room with this little hellion. What was she supposed to do if he screamed all night? This wasn't what she had planned at all.

"Oh, dear," Lucy said, coming back into the living room and scooping Sam out of Jessica's arms. "Naughty boy," she crooned, kissing him over and over again. "Naughty little Sambo."

Jessica felt sick. Sam kept bawling, and the little house suddenly felt suffocatingly small.

But there was always the prospect of Tony, she reminded herself. Not that this was exactly the sort of place she pictured a big star like Tony visiting, but still . . . family was family.

"Let me show you where the nursery is

again," Josh said over the din of Sam's crying. Jessica followed him through the narrow hallway to the baby's room, which was now extremely crowded with Jessica's mountain of luggage.

"As we told you before, we did think about putting you in the guest room, but we thought . . . you know, in case Sam cries during the night," Josh apologized, following her crestfallen gaze.

Jessica gulped. "Of course," she said brightly. "Besides, you probably want to keep the guest room free," she added knowingly.

Josh smiled but shook his head, puzzled. "Why's that?"

"Oh, you know." Jessica sounded vague. "In case any of your relatives come to visit. Like Tony." She put all the meaning she was capable of into the name.

"Tony?" Josh stared at her. "Oh, you mean my cousin?"

Jessica suddenly felt faint. Something about Josh's blank stare gave her the distinct impression that a visit from Tony wasn't imminent.

"Oh, Tony's too busy to visit us these days. Being a star takes up all his time. I haven't seen him since Lucy and I got married three summers ago!"

"Oh," Jessica said. "Oh, well."

"I'll just leave you to get settled," Josh said, smiling broadly at her.

Jessica nodded dumbly. The minute he left she turned to look around her with dismay—the small crib, the fold-out cot . . .

Five

"This," Lila said happily, tossing a lock of long, light brown hair off her shoulders, "is the life. Aren't you glad I convinced you to come to Malibu, Jess?"

Jessica stared at the sparkling blue sea before her. "No," she snapped, brushing at an invisible fleck of sand on her smooth brown leg.

She and Lila were stretched out on the public beach bordering the Bennets' property, waiting for Elizabeth to arrive with little Taryn. The girls had all arranged to get Mondays off so they could do things together. But Monday seemed a long way off just then to Jessica. Six whole days away, in fact. Luckily she had managed to convince Lucy that Sam's nap time was a good time for her to go out for a jog. "I just hope Sam sleeps for at least four hours," Jessica grumbled. "I'm going crazy being cooped up in that tiny house!"

Lila smiled sympathetically. "I don't see how you stand it," she agreed. "Why don't you get Liz to trade with you, Jess? She doesn't care about things like space, does she?"

Jessica's aqua eyes widened. Then she shook her head. "I couldn't do that," she said finally. "After I dragged her all the way here."

"Why not?" Lila demanded. "Liz is so good-natured she'd probably be happy to switch if you just asked her nicely."

Jessica sighed. "Liz may be good-natured, but she's not stupid. It's like living in a playpen over at the Sargents'! The whole house is bursting with baby stuff. I don't even think I like babies," she added. "Don't you hate changing diapers?"

Lila looked horror-stricken. *"Diapers?* I don't do that!" she exclaimed. "The *nurse* does that. All I do is play with Mikey after he's had his nap." Lila took a fat paperback out of her bag. "The only thing *I* have to worry about," she pointed out, "is when we're going to meet some of these gorgeous guys I keep seeing all over the place. Malibu is just swarming with wonderful men—and I want to get my hands on one of them!"

"Men," Jessica said moodily. "Lila, you sound like you're about twenty-five. Aren't you interested in just plain *boys* anymore?"

"Boys," Lila said disdainfully, "are too child-ish." She opened her paperback, read for a minute or two, and then looked up, her brown eyes dreamy. "I want to meet a guy like the hero in this book." She waved it at Jessica. "His name is Rock Owens. He has everything: looks, money, a couple of villas in Europe. . . . Listen to this!"

Jessica rolled her eyes, then flipped over on her stomach as Lila read aloud.

" 'Rock was tall and swarthy. His dark eyes flashed like fire in his tanned face. The minute Elinore saw him she knew this was it . . . he was the one. The muscles rippled in his arms as he raised her to him, his manly face filled with passion. "Kiss me, Rock!" Elinore moaned softly.' "

Jessica groaned. "That's ridiculous," she said. "Lila, your problem is that you're never willing to compromise. You're never going to meet some millionaire named Rock! You have to, you know, spend a little more time on this planet."

Lila set her book down, her face determined. "I just need an older man," she told her friend. "Someone mature, someone who's already been through the kind of stuff we're going through now. Trust me, Jess. This is going to be the sum-mer I find him."

"Hey," Jessica said, sitting up a little straighter, her eyes narrowed. "Speaking of finding someone, *that's* the sort of guy *I'd* like to meet." She gave a low whistle of admiration as she watched a tall, well-built blond jogging toward them along the edge of the water.

Lila looked on with interest. "Not bad," she admitted. "But don't you think he looks . . . I don't know, kind of boyish?"

Jessica giggled. "You forget," she teased her friend, "you're the one who's looking for Mr. Rock of Ages—not me!" She adjusted herself carefully on her straw mat, crossing her slender legs at the ankle and shaking back her hair so it tumbled around her shoulders. The boy was getting closer, and she wanted to look her best. "Hey," Jessica whispered excitedly, "don't look now, but he's heading over here!"

To Jessica's profound disappointment, the boy jogged right past them. She could have sworn he'd been watching her as he got closer, but he didn't stop.

"Darn," Jessica said, scooping up a handful of sand and letting it run through her fingers. "*I* think he's gorgeous." She watched the muscles working in his legs as he loped off toward the lighthouse. "I wish—"

Her reverie was interrupted by the cheerful sound of Elizabeth's voice, hailing them from the Bennets' redwood deck. "We're on our way down!" Elizabeth called. Jessica shaded her eyes. She could see Taryn on the deck, too, her tiny face screwed up in a pout.

"I think poor Liz has her hands full with that brat," Jessica said. She shot Lila a glance. "Maybe," she said slyly, "I'd be doing *her* a favor if I asked her to swap jobs."

Lila giggled. "Now you're talking."

"Hi," Elizabeth said breathlessly several minutes later. She was loaded with all of Taryn's beach things; plastic bucket, miniature folding chair, blanket, umbrella, and a doll dressed in a bathing suit.

"Hi, Taryn." Lila leaned over to give the girl her most artificial smile.

Taryn frowned at her. "I want to go back inside," she said to Elizabeth and stuck her thumb in her mouth.

"Come on, Taryn," Elizabeth said cheerfully, dropping some of the toys on the sand while she arranged the blanket and umbrella. "It's such a pretty day. Why would you want to go back inside?"

"Because," Taryn said sullenly. She kept her thumb in her mouth, which made her lisp and sound younger than her six years.

"We're going to have fun out here," Elizabeth insisted, but there was a note of uncertainty in her voice. "I thought you said you wanted to play with your bucket. I thought we were going to make a sand castle!"

"I don't want to make a sand castle." Taryn took her thumb out of her mouth. "I don't like you," she said clearly, looking straight at Elizabeth. "I want you to go away."

"Well, I like *you*, Taryn," Elizabeth said, sighing. Taryn turned and walked toward the water. "Something tells me I'm doing something wrong," she mused.

Jessica and Lila exchanged amused glances. "I get the impression Taryn isn't exactly president of the Elizabeth Wakefield Fan Club," Jessica said. Seeing the concerned expression on her sister's face, she quickly changed her tone. "Don't worry," she assured her. "The kid's a spoiled brat. What does it matter what she thinks?"

"I feel sorry for her." Elizabeth slipped out of her T-shirt, revealing a pretty navy one-piece. "I can't believe the kind of life she has! Maria is more like a mother to her than her real mother is. She barely ever sees her parents."

"She still seems like a brat to me," Jessica said. "I don't know how you can stand it."

"Well, we've only been here a few days," Elizabeth reminded her. "Give me time. I may lose my cool yet!"

"Speaking of losing your cool," Lila said, yawning extravagantly, "your twin has just fallen madly in love with a mysterious blond jogger. Hold her back, Liz. She's on the verge of chasing him down."

50

"Really?" Elizabeth was curious. "Where is this hunk?"

"He went that way," Jessica said mournfully, pointing down the beach. "He passed right by us, but he didn't stop."

"It's all right. You're going to have a second chance. I think I see him coming back!" Lila pushed Jessica playfully. "Do something dramatic when he comes past us this time—like trip him!"

"Hey, I know him," Elizabeth said, shading her eyes with her hand. "That's Cliff Sherman!"

"Cliff Sherman?" Jessica bounced on her straw mat. "How do *you* know him, Liz?" She didn't know whether to shout with joy at her luck or to despair because her twin had gotten to him first.

"He lives next door to the Bennets," Elizabeth said matter-of-factly. "Don't worry," she added, seeing the grieved expression on her sister's face. "I'm not interested in him, Jess. He's all yours!"

Jessica reddened. "I just—I mean, how did you meet him? Is he nice? How old is he? Where—"

"Whoa!" Elizabeth laughed and held up a hand. "One question at a time!" Taryn had been walking toward them, a bucket of wet sand in her hands. Now she halted and sat down in the sand. Elizabeth smiled encouragingly at her.

"Come up and keep us company!" she called, trying to ignore the scowl on the little girl's face.

Elizabeth shrugged. "He's on the beach a lot. He seems really nice. He just graduated from high school, but he doesn't know if he's going to go to college in California or out of state. He's really friendly. I'm sure it'll be easy for you to get to know him. That's his parents' house." She pointed up to a lofty redwood house on the lot next to the Bennets'.

"Look," Lila said out of the corner of her mouth. "I think he's jogging your way, Jess."

Jessica's eyes sparkled as Cliff bounced to a slow jog, then a walk. "Hi, Taryn," he said, bending over to rumple the little girl's hair. "Hi, Liz!" He strolled toward them, wiping his brow.

Up close, Cliff was even cuter than Jessica had thought.

"Cliff, this is my sister, Jessica, and our friend Lila Fowler," Elizabeth said.

"Hey, there are two of you!" Cliff's eyes brightened as he dropped down on the sand next to the girls. "I thought you were Liz at first," he said to Jessica. "I was going to stop and say hello, but I figured if I stopped I'd never start again."

"Do you run every day?" Jessica asked, her eyes warmly appreciative.

"Five miles," Cliff told her.

Lila groaned. "I couldn't even run a mile!"

Jessica gave her a dirty look. "I love to jog," she fibbed, ignoring Elizabeth's wink at Lila. "I think it's the best way to keep in shape. We should run together sometime," she added.

Cliff laughed. His teeth were straight and bright white. "I'm not really very good company when I'm running. But actually, I was wondering if you three have plans for this Saturday night. I've got a friend coming down from San Francisco for a few weeks, and I'm throwing a big party for him. It should be a blast, a big barbecue on the beach, dancing—"

"I think it sounds wonderful," Jessica said quickly. "I'd love to come, Cliff."

Lila nodded emphatically. "Count me in, too. I can't wait to meet some more people around here."

"Well, this'll be a good chance for that," Cliff affirmed. "I'll make sure you meet everyone."

Jessica lowered her lashes meaningfully. "I'll be looking forward to it," she said, trying to inject special significance into her words. Cliff smiled as he got to his feet. "Great! See you all on Saturday night, then, around eight o'clock. OK?"

Elizabeth didn't answer. She was watching in horror as Taryn proceeded to scoop up a huge lump of wet sand with her little plastic shovel and drop it on Cliff's running shoe.

"Thanks, Taryn," Cliff said dryly, kicking the

sand off and shaking his head at her. "Take care of her, Liz," he admonished.

"Taryn," Elizabeth scolded.

But there was no getting through to the little girl. "I hate him," Taryn said fiercely, rubbing her tear-filled eyes with her knuckles. "And I hate you, too!"

Elizabeth stood up as Taryn began to run away toward the house. "I'll be back in a sec!" She set off in pursuit.

Jessica was oblivious to this minidrama. She was absorbed instead by the sight of Cliff Sherman walking up the beach toward his own house.

The Bennets' situation had looked attractive enough before. But now that Jessica knew Cliff Sherman was part of the package, she wouldn't rest a single minute until she had done everything in her power to convince Elizabeth to switch jobs with her for the rest of the summer!

Six

At first Jessica wasn't sure what had woken her up. Then she heard Sam crying, and she remembered where she was. The digital clock next to her bed said 6:00 A.M., and even though the sky was already getting light, it felt to Jessica as though it were the middle of the night.

"OK, OK," she groaned, swinging her legs over the side of the bed and rubbing her eyes. A baby was a million times worse than an alarm clock, she thought unhappily. At least you could turn off a clock, at least push the snooze button. But there was no turning little Sam off. He was ready for his bottle, and until he got it, he was bound to keep crying his head off.

By now this early-morning routine was familiar to Jessica. Half-asleep, she stumbled around the tiny room, putting on her bathrobe and scooping Sam out of his crib. His crying stopped for a moment when she lifted him, then began again, louder than ever. "I know you're hungry," Jessica told him, shaking her head at the furious look on his tiny face. "I'm moving as fast as I can, OK?" Still holding him, she tiptoed down the dark hallway to the kitchen, took a bottle of formula out of the refrigerator, and turned on the stove to heat it.

When the bottle was ready, Jessica sat down at the kitchen table to feed Sam, her eyes surveying the scene around her with distaste. Lucy and Josh were really nice people, but they sure seemed casual about the way they lived! Not that Jessica was that neat herself. At home she was always defending herself against criticism about her room, which Jessica thought of as "comfortable" and the rest of the family declared a total disaster area. But Jessica's room was one thing. The rest of the Wakefield house was neat as a pin, whereas the Sargents' house was messy *everywhere*!

But messiness alone wouldn't have discouraged Jessica. The main problem was that the Sargents' house was too far from the beach—and from Cliff Sherman. Otherwise, she didn't mind her job that much. Sam kept strange hours, but he wasn't very much trouble, and Lucy was wonderful about letting Jessica slip off in the afternoons to meet Lila and Elizabeth.

Jessica looked down at the contented expression on the baby's face as he drank from his bottle and thought about the conversation she had had on the phone with Elizabeth the night before. Unfortunately, she hadn't been thrilled when Jessica had volunteered to exchange jobs with her. "No, thanks," she had retorted immediately. "I may be a pushover, but I'm not a sucker, Jess. I'm perfectly happy at the Bennets'."

Jessica had tried every angle she could think of. She reminded Elizabeth of how obnoxious Taryn was and how much stricter the Bennets were about everything. But Elizabeth refused to acknowledge her generosity. "Wild horses couldn't convince me to switch" was all she would say, much to Lila's amusement and Jessica's disappointment.

Well, Jessica thought, she was just going to have to try something a little more subtle. If Elizabeth was going to be stubborn, she would simply redouble her efforts! There was no way Jessica could sit by and let Elizabeth keep the Bennets' job, not when it meant living next door to Cliff Sherman.

"Good morning," Lucy said from the doorway, interrupting Jessica's thoughts. "How's my baby?" She patted Sam's tiny foot and yawned.

"Do you want some coffee?" she asked Jessica, taking a canister out of the refrigerator.

"No, thanks," Jessica said, shifting Sam in her arms. She couldn't help being a little disappointed that Lucy was already up. Jessica felt like being alone. She wanted to daydream about Cliff and count the days until his party on Saturday. It was already Wednesday—only three days more to go!

A few minutes later the coffee was brewing, and Lucy sat down at the table and smiled at her baby. Lucy was one of those women who looked good, even first thing in the morning, with no makeup on. At least Jessica thought Lucy was pretty, with her red hair and soft brown eyes. "Tell me how things are going for you," Lucy said, getting up to pour a cup of coffee when the brewer's "ready" light went on. "Are you having a good time, making any friends?"

"Well, I met a guy yesterday," Jessica confided. "He's gorgeous, Lucy. He has really blond hair and the best build! He lives right next to the Bennets'. Do you know the house? It's redwood and has a big back porch?"

"Oh, you mean the Shermans," Lucy said, taking a sip of coffee. She wiggled her fingers at Sam and smiled. "They're really nice people. I know who Cliff is. You're right. He *is* cute."

Jessica shifted a little. Sam was beginning to feel heavy on her lap. "Anyway, he's having a party this Saturday night, and he's invited all of us—Lila and Liz and me. I can't wait. It sounds like it'll be great!"

"It sure does!" Lucy said. The next minute a shadow crossed her face. "Wait a minute—this Saturday?" she asked. "Oh, Jess, I feel terrible, but Josh and I have plans. We're going to a friend's house for dinner. I'd say we could switch it, but it's kind of a big deal. This man asked us ages ago, and I'm afraid—"

Jessica stared at her, crestfallen. "You mean—"

"I'm afraid we're really going to need you to stay here with Sam," Lucy finished, sighing. "I'm really sorry, Jess. If I could find someone else to sit for him, we'd be all set, but I can't think of anyone. Can you?"

Jessica blinked in disbelief. Her dreams were being dashed before her very eyes! She *had* to go to Cliff's party on Saturday, that was all there was to it. "Maybe I can find someone," she said doubtfully, staring intently at little Sam so Lucy wouldn't see the tears welling in her eyes.

She knew Lucy and Josh had every right to go out whenever they chose. Part of her job was to be available when they needed her. She just couldn't believe her own rotten luck. The best-looking guy around was going to be waiting for her to show up on Saturday night.

And unless she did something drastic, Jessica

was going to be sitting home at the Sargents', changing diapers and heating up formula while the first big party of the summer went on without her!

"You *have* to feel like doing *something*," Elizabeth said reasonably, shaking her head as she looked around Taryn's bedroom. She couldn't get over how many toys the little girl had—closet after closet filled with games and dolls. But Taryn wasn't interested in any of them.

"We could go to the beach," Elizabeth said hopefully, looking longingly out the window at the sparkling blue sea.

Taryn stuck her lower lip out. "I don't want to."

Elizabeth sighed for what she was sure was the millionth time. This was a lot harder than she had expected. She had tried every tactic she could think of to bring Taryn out of her shell, but the child remained aloof and disagreeable. She made it clear she hated Elizabeth and hated every activity Elizabeth suggested.

If it weren't for Taryn's perpetual pout, she would have been a beautiful little girl, Elizabeth thought. She had short, soft black hair and big violet-blye eyes fringed with dark lashes. Her clothing, of course, was impeccable. She had dozens of pretty dresses, chest after chest filled with beautiful clothing. Like a doll, Elizabeth thought sadly, because it was increasingly clear to her that Audrey Bennet treated her only child more like a doll than a daughter.

Elizabeth had never met people like the Bennets. They were incredibly glamorous, both of them, but they weren't affectionate—to each other *or* to their little girl. Malcolm Bennet came from a very wealthy family and seemed to care more about maintaining his image among the well-to-do Malibu set than anything else. He drove the white Jaguar Elizabeth had seen the day she came for her interview, and he spent a great deal of time fussing over the car, worrying about little noises no one else could hear. The rest of the time he was at "the club," the Malibu Polo Club. Maria said Mr. Bennet played cards there and occasionally golfed. "But what about work?" Elizabeth asked her, confused.

"Oh," Maria had replied, shrugging, "he always takes it easy in the summer. He's a private investor, and things are always slower in the summer months."

Elizabeth found it all very strange. Mrs. Bennet mystified Elizabeth even more than her husband. She was several years younger than he was and strikingly beautiful, with jet black hair and the same clear, violet-blue eyes as Taryn.

She was very tall—almost six feet—and model slim. Her clothes took Elizabeth's breath away.

Elizabeth wanted to like Mrs. Bennet, but it was hard. For one thing, Mrs. Bennet was cool and remote whenever they spoke. She always seemed to be rushing off somewhere. She met friends for lunch, but the bulk of her time as far as Elizabeth could tell was spent either shopping or at the spa. Maria confided that Audrey Bennet was a fitness freak, obsessed about her figure. She swam hundreds of laps every day in addition to taking exercise classes.

No wonder poor Taryn was so unhappy, Elizabeth thought. She hardly ever saw either her mom or her dad, and Elizabeth suspected that when she did she was acutely aware that something was wrong between them. Children could be so much more sensitive to family tensions than adults, and Taryn, for all her stubborn belligerence, struck Elizabeth as an extremely smart little girl.

But a lonely one. She had no friends, was never allowed to go to other children's homes. With Maria and Emily, the cook, she acted spoiled and sullen—as she did with Elizabeth. But Elizabeth was almost positive she misbehaved out of misery. The poor thing didn't know how to reach out to anyone. She didn't really know what affection was!

Still, for all her good intentions, Elizabeth

couldn't help sometimes getting impatient. She hadn't been there a week, yet she found herself living for the afternoons, when she, Lila, and Jessica managed to join one another on the beach.

Elizabeth couldn't help recalling from time to time that she had given up a perfectly nice summer in Sweet Valley—a productive summer at the *News*—for this. Still, she wasn't one to second-guess her choices. She was here, and she was determined to make the best of it.

"Come on, Taryn. We're going to do something fun," Elizabeth said firmly. "Let's go down to the beach and swim."

"You always want to go to the beach," Taryn complained, but she allowed Elizabeth to help her into her bathing suit, one of about a dozen. After what seemed to Elizabeth like ages, they were finally ready and heading out into the brilliant sunshine of a Malibu summer.

"Look how tanned you're getting, Taryn," Elizabeth commented as she held her arm next to the girl's to compare their skin color.

Taryn skipped away. "There's your dumb old sister," she shouted, pointing down the beach with her shovel.

Elizabeth squinted. Sure enough, Jessica was trudging toward them, her shoulders slumped.

"Where're you going?" Elizabeth called after Taryn.

"Over there." Taryn was making her way to a grassy knoll a few dozen yards off.

By that point Jessica had reached her sister. She threw herself down on the sand, an expression of dire misery on her face.

"What's wrong with *you*?" Elizabeth demanded. "Gosh, between you and Taryn I'm really getting drowned in bad moods today!"

Jessica sat up and looked hard at her twin. "You know, Liz, I really would be willing to swap jobs with you. I wasn't just saying that to be nice last night."

Elizabeth laughed. "I did get the impression you really meant what you said. But I told you, Jess, there's no way. Even if I wanted to, I wouldn't do it. It wouldn't be very professional."

Jessica stared hopelessly at her. "Forget it." She turned away to stare listlessly at the ocean.

"What's wrong?" Elizabeth looked worried. "Is something the matter at the Sargents'? Are they giving you too much work?"

Jessica shook her head. "No . . . it's just . . . oh, never mind." She sighed and put her head in her hands. "I'll get over it. It's no big deal."

"Over what?" Elizabeth demanded.

"Cliff's party," Jessica said tragically. Taking a deep breath, she proceeded to explain the entire situation to her sister.

Elizabeth frowned. "Jess, that's terrible. You

64

were really looking forward to that party, weren't you?"

"Yeah," Jessica mumbled. "But who cares. So what if I never get to see Cliff again. What difference does it make?"

"Look." Elizabeth looked sympathetically at her twin. "I haven't had a chance yet to ask the Bennets if they're doing anything that night. If they're not, I'll sit for Sam. I don't mind missing the party."

"You don't?" Jessica shrieked. "Oh, Liz, did I ever tell you how much I love you?"

Elizabeth laughed. "Remember, I have to ask the Bennets first. They may need me to stay with Taryn."

But there was no dampening Jessica's enthusiasm. "You," she said emphatically, "are the world's best sister, and the next time you need a favor, whatever it is, you know who to turn to!"

Elizabeth shook her head. "Remember, though, this is the last time," she said warningly.

It was hard to tell whether Jessica realized she meant it or not. Elizabeth hoped so. She had her work cut out for her as it was this summer. The last thing she needed was to start taking on Jessica's responsibilities as well as her own!

Seven

"So Liz really refuses to swap jobs?" Lila and Jessica were strolling through the small, elegant Palm Mall in nearby Santa Monica, where they had driven to do some shopping. It was Thursday, and Lucy had told Jessica that she could take the afternoon off. Lila, of course, could take off whenever she felt like it.

"She says she wouldn't do it in a million years," Jessica said, stopping to admire a dress in a shop window. "But I'm not convinced. At first I thought she really meant it, but then . . . well, after she agreed to sit for Sam on Saturday, I started thinking—maybe she just needs a little subtle persuasion."

"What do you mean?"

"Well, I guess asking her straight out if she

would switch with me wasn't a good idea. What I'm thinking is that I may need to make her feel seriously sorry for me, make her think I really can't handle life at the Sargents'."

"How are you going to do that?" Lila raised an eyebrow skeptically.

"Well, Plan A is that disgusting cat the Sargents have. Can you imagine naming a cat Spot?" Jessica wrinkled her nose. "I can't stand that thing!"

"Jess," Lila objected, "Liz is hardly going to trade jobs with you just because you don't like the Sargents' *cat*."

"True," Jessica said. "But what if I convince her I'm allergic? Liz is too good a sister to make me sweat out the whole summer with a cat, especially if I start sneezing all the time and complain about getting rashes!"

Lila shook her head. "It sounds pretty desperate to me. I think you'd better make yourself good and comfortable at the Sargents'."

"You just don't know my persuasive powers." Jessica giggled. "Lila, come into this store with me. I want to try on that dress. Don't you think it's perfect for Cliff's party?"

"It depends," Lila said dryly. "Are you going to have a rash by then?"

The two entered the store. Jessica found the dress in a size six and slipped into a dressing room. "I'm going back out," Lila announced, yawning. If *she* wasn't doing the shopping, she wasn't interested.

"Stay with me and tell me how it looks." Jessica's voice was muffled under the folds of fabric. But Lila had already wandered away, her eye on a jewelry store right across the mall's courtyard.

Her mind only partly on the brightly colored gems in the window, Lila was humming to herself while she waited for Jessica to emerge. Suddenly a low male voice broke into her reverie.

"I know this sounds stupid, but haven't I seen you someplace before?"

Lila spun around, surprised. A tall boy in chinos and a forest-green polo shirt was sitting on a marble bench several feet away. He was clean-cut and not at all bad looking, with auburn hair and hazel eyes. Lila found his intelligent, urbane manner instantly appealing.

She blushed slightly. "I—uh, I don't think so. I'm not even from around here."

He laughed. "That's funny! Neither am I. I'm from San Francisco. My name's Ben Horgan. What's yours?"

Lila stared at him, Ordinarily she would have been insulted by this kind of straightforward approach from a total stranger, but there was something likable about him. "Lila Fowler," she said, quickly lowering her eyes. When she looked up again, he was smiling at her, a frank, friendly smile.

"Where are you from, Lila?" he asked casually, putting down the newspaper he had been reading.

"From Sweet Valley," Lila said. "I'm here for the summer. I'm a mother's helper for a family in Malibu."

"Really?" He looked interested. "I'm staying with friends in Malibu. Where are—"

"Lila!" Jessica called from inside the dress shop. "Come tell me how this looks!"

Lila looked at Ben with embarrassment. "My friend," she said lamely. "I guess I better go."

"Have you ever wind surfed?" Ben asked. Lila shook her head. "I'm a wonderful coach." He smiled warmly at her. "We could meet on the beach sometime tomorrow—if you're not busy with your job, that is."

Lila thought it over. Why not? She could see Jessica moving around inside the dress shop, admiring herself in the dress before a three-way mirror. "Let's meet in front of the lifeguard's chair at the public beach at one o'clock," she suggested.

"Great! I'll see you then."

Lila hurried away, her cheeks burning. What a wonderful guy! He was so friendly, so laid back, so . . . *mature*, she thought happily. Not like the guys back home at all. It was hard to tell how old he was—eighteen? Nineteen? Definitely the suave, sophisticated type. None of the guys in her class at school would ever dare start a conversation with her that way!

"What do you think?" Jessica asked, twirling around.

"Not bad. You should take it," Lila said absently, her mind still on Ben.

Jessica looked at the price tag and sighed. "When I think how many diapers I'll have to change for this . . ."

Lila wrinkled her nose. "Don't be so gross, Jess." It didn't take much persuading before Jessica had taken the dress to the cash register.

"Who was that guy I saw you talking to?" Jessica asked, turning back to Lila with curiosity.

Lila's brown eyes brightened. "I thought you'd never ask." Taking a deep breath, she began to fill her friend in on the guy she'd just decided was going to be the object of her summer romance.

"Ahh-choo!" Jessica sneezed as dramatically as she could, making little Taryn's blue eyes widen. Elizabeth, absorbed in the letter she had just received from Enid, didn't seem to notice.

"What are you doing that for?" Taryn asked solemnly, looking up at Jessica from the spot where she was filling a hole in the sand with muddy water.

"Doing what for?" Jessica was trying to make her eyes water by squinting at the sun.

"Sneezing that way. You look funny," Taryn said.

Jessica frowned. "You'd better not say I look funny, Taryn, or something bad might happen."

Taryn looked at her, intrigued. "Like what?" she demanded.

Jessica leaned over, out of Elizabeth's earshot. "Listen," she whispered. "Don't you know what happens to wicked little girls?"

Taryn shook her head, round-eyed. "What?" she whispered back.

Jessica eyed her seriously. "Once upon a time," she whispered, "there was a wicked little girl named Taryn. She was so wicked that one day she was just minding her own business, being wicked, and an enormous frog came by and swallowed her. And that was it."

Taryn's mouth dropped open. "Are you sure?" She raised her voice anxiously.

"What's going on, you two?" Elizabeth had been chuckling at a passage in the letter. Now she put it aside reluctantly.

Jessica winked at Taryn. "Secrets," she said mysteriously. "Right, Taryn?"

Taryn just stared at Jessica in fascination.

Jessica blinked extravagantly. "Ahh-ahhchoooo!" she shrieked, grabbing theatrically at a pocket-size pack of tissues.

"Jess, what's wrong with you?" Elizabeth asked, concerned. "Are you getting sick?"

Jessica's turquoise eyes widened innocently. "Sick? Oh, am I sneezing again? Darn," she added, dabbing at her nose. "It must still be that silly cat."

"What cat?" Elizabeth asked suspiciously.

"You know—Spot, the Sargents' cat. I guess I must be allergic or something. I've just been sneezing and sneezing." Jessica blew her nose forcefully, sitting down in the sand as if that last sneeze had drained her of all her remaining strength.

"That's funny," Elizabeth said. "Didn't you have allergy tests a few years ago, when you thought you were allergic to dishwashing soap?"

"Really? I don't remember," Jessica said.

Elizabeth's blond ponytail bounced as she nodded emphatically. "I do. You kept insisting you were allergic, so Mom made you go through all those horrible tests. Anyway, you weren't allergic to anything."

Jessica reached for another tissue. "Some allergies develop late in life," she reminded Elizabeth. "I think my allergy to Spot must be the late-developing kind."

Elizabeth looked closely at her and laughed.

"Something tells me you're right," she said dryly.

Jessica sniffed delicately. "Liz, I really appreciate your sitting for Sam this Saturday. Are you sure it's all right with the Bennets?"

"They don't mind at all," Elizabeth said, picking her letter up again. "They're going out, but they're planning to take Taryn with them."

Taryn picked up a stick and began to draw in the sand. "I don't want to go," she whispered to herself.

"What's that, Taryn?" Elizabeth asked.

Taryn shook her head, refusing to answer.

"So, anyway, it's fine," Elizabeth told Jessica. "I'll be over at the Sargents' around eight." She frowned and changed the subject. "Mom called me last night. She sounds like she's really missing us."

Jessica sighed. "I miss her, too." She sniffed loudly. "It's so hard for me over at the Sargents', Liz. I'm not kidding. I mean, having to get up every morning at six o'clock, and changing all those diapers . . ."

"Whose idea was this?" Elizabeth remarked.

Jessica was quiet for a minute. "You know, I don't think I'm very good with babies," she said, plucking a tiny gull feather off the oversize aqua cotton T-shirt she wore knotted at her hips for a cover-up. "In fact I think I'm kind of scared, taking care of Sam. I'd really feel much better about a child who was a little older."

"I'm sure you're doing a great job with Sam," Elizabeth assured her with a smile. "I wouldn't worry about it, Jess. It's only a summer job. Enid sounds like *she's* having a great summer," she added, trying to change the subject.

"But I'm really scared of him," Jessica protested. "I'm always absolutely convinced that I'm going to drop him!"

Elizabeth shook her head. "Jess, it isn't working," she said firmly, putting Enid's letter away and reaching for her novel.

"The Sargents are really literary sort of people." Jessica peeked over Elizabeth's shoulder at her book. "I think they feel really disappointed that I can't talk about literature with them. Maybe—"

"*Jess*," Elizabeth said emphatically.

Taryn had listened to this whole exchange with interest. "Jessica," she said, coming over to stand right next to her and putting a hand shyly on her arm, "tell me another secret."

Jessica stared at her in surprise. "OK," she said. She thought for a minute, then cupped her hand around Taryn's ear. "Once there was a *really* wicked little girl named Taryn," she whispered. Taryn giggled, delighted. "She was *so* wicked that she turned into a dollar bill, without even realizing what had happened to her, and

75

the next thing she knew, someone came along and spent her!"

"Tell me another," Taryn begged.

Elizabeth was watching with fascination. "Jess, what *is* your secret?" she demanded.

Jessica's eyes sparkled. "Taryn and I are on the same wavelength, aren't we, Taryn?" she said.

The little girl nodded emphatically, and Jessica felt a sudden surge of hope. It was obvious Elizabeth wasn't going to change jobs out of sympathy for Jessica.

But what if Jessica could convince her it would be better for Taryn if Jessica were to spend the rest of the summer at the Bennets'?

Eight

"You're pretty good," Ben called out, shaking his head and laughing as little droplets of water flew in all directions.

"Thanks," Lila said lightly, running up out of the waves to join Ben on the beach. She hadn't bothered mentioning the special class she'd taken in wind surfing the summer before. Better to let Ben believe his own expertise had been at work all afternoon and that she was just an incredibly quick learner!

Lila couldn't help admiring Ben's bronzed physique in his plaid bathing suit. He was really a good-looking guy—a little more clean-cut than some of the boys she'd dated, and definitely more sophisticated. He had been entertaining her with stories about his exciting life in San

Francisco. No doubt about it, Lila thought, Sweet Valley couldn't compete.

"How would you like to go out to a movie tonight?" she asked him a few minutes later, when they were positioned on their towels, drying in the sunlight. Lila tried to sit so her legs showed to their best advantage. She had to admit she was getting a knockout tan from so many hours on the beach.

Ben cleared his throat. "Tonight? Uh—tonight might be kind of difficult. My car is in the shop," he blurted quickly.

Lila raised her eyebrows. "We can take my car," she offered.

Ben didn't answer for a minute. "OK," he said at last. Something was wrong, but Lila couldn't think what it might be. "We could just go for a walk instead," Ben said suddenly, his face brightening. "There aren't any good movies in town, anyway."

Lila felt embarrassed. Obviously Ben had already seen the two movies she had hoped to see. "Fine," she said quickly. "Let's meet right here. We can just walk and look at the water."

Ben seemed to be relieved. "You know, I think you're my kind of girl," he said huskily, leaning forward to stare deep into her eyes. "The sort of girl who would rather stroll under the moonlight than sit in a small-town movie theater."

Lila opened her mouth to defend Malibu, but

before she could speak, Ben was leaning closer. The next thing she knew his warm lips were brushing hers, and Lila forgot all about Malibu and the movies. All she could think about was how good it felt to kiss Ben.

Suddenly she was sure he was right. A moon-lit walk was better than the movies any day!

"He sounds wonderful," Jessica said. She and Lila were curled up in front of the television set in the Sargents' cluttered living room. Lucy and Josh were at Lucy's parents' house, and Jessica was baby-sitting for little Sam, who was merci-fully exhausted after a long day and had just fallen asleep. "Is he in high school in San Francisco, or college?"

"He didn't say." Lila reached for a potato chip. "I'm pretty sure he must be a freshman in college at the very least. He's really mature, Jessica. None of this babyish high-school stuff."

"When are you going to see him again?" Jessica was vicariously thrilled by Lila's new romance. "You should invite him to Cliff's party tomorrow night!"

"I'm meeting him on the beach at nine tonight," Lila said airily. "We'll probably make plans to see each other again soon. But I'm not sure he'd really fit in at Cliff's party. He's very grown-up."

Jessica wrinkled her forehead. "Is he boring?"

"No! I didn't mean *that*." Lila described Ben's reaction when she'd suggested a movie. "I just don't think he likes really ordinary things like that," she concluded. "He's terribly romantic."

"Oh, well," Jessica said. "Wait a minute. Does that mean you're not coming with me tomorrow night?"

Lila shrugged. "I'll probably come," she said. "Unless Ben has something else in mind. I guess it's not a good idea to rush things right at the beginning, anyway. Especially not with someone who's really been around, like Ben."

Jessica giggled. "You make him sound like he's about fifty!" Personally Jessica couldn't imagine anything worse than a guy who was too old to enjoy parties and movies. *She* couldn't wait for Cliff's party! The new dress was hanging in the little closet in Sam's room, all ready for her to slip into the next night. She knew she was going to look sensational. Already her tan was much deeper, and the creamy white of the dress would show it off perfectly.

Jessica had run into Cliff only once after the time they'd met on the beach. As a matter of fact, it had been that very morning, Friday. She had taken Sam out in his stroller and had ended up walking all the way into town. Lucy had mentioned needing a few things from the grocery store, and Jessica, feeling a sudden surge of good will now that she was convinced she wouldn't be working for the Sargents much longer, decided to buy the eggs and butter with her own money. She was halfway down the dairy aisle when she saw Cliff coming straight toward her, a six-pack of sodas in his hand.

"Hi!" Cliff had smiled broadly at her. "I can tell you're Jessica," he'd said teasingly, "unless little Taryn shrunk about ten sizes."

"This is Sam Sargent," Jessica had told him, leaning over to squeeze Sam's bare foot. Sam made a burbling noise. Jessica had felt embarrassed meeting Cliff again in such a domestic setting. There she was with a baby stroller and a little basket of groceries. But Cliff was incredibly friendly.

"You're still planning on coming tomorrow night, aren't you?" he'd asked her, carrying her groceries for her as they headed together to the checkout counter.

Jessica had nodded, feeling suddenly shy. "I'm looking forward to it," she told him, wishing she were wearing something a little more special. Her white shorts and tank top seemed plain.

But Cliff didn't seem to notice. "I'm glad," he had said with a smile, his eyes fixed penetratingly on hers. "Too bad you won't be able to come, little guy," he had added, patting Sam on the head. "But I'm sure glad your baby-sitter is around here this summer."

Jessica had glowed all day after that comment. She could barely wait till the next night. She kept thinking of herself in her beautiful new dress, dancing dreamily in Cliff's strong arms. She wondered what it would feel like the first time he kissed her. . . .

"You're not even listening to me," Lila complained.

Jessica sat up with a start. "Sorry," she said. "Give me another chance. What did you say?"

"I *asked* you what the deal is with changing jobs!" Lila munched another handful of chips. "Did your allergy trick work? Does Liz feel sorry for you?"

"It was a total flop," Jessica admitted cheerfully. "And I mean *total.* She didn't buy it for a single second. I forgot I went through complete allergy tests a few years ago. I wasn't allergic to so much as a stuffed cat!"

Lila giggled. "What are you going to do now? Don't tell me you'd resign yourself to a summer here!" She grimaced at the tiny living room.

Jessica looked horrified. "What? And let Liz live next door to Cliff when she doesn't even like him? That would be *too* unfair! No way. I have another plan."

"What is it this time? Are you going to plant

yourself at the Bennets', claim you're Liz, and insist she's got amnesia?"

Jessica blinked. "That's not such a bad idea," she said, reaching for a can of soda.

Lila shook her head. "You're a maniac, you know that?"

"No, I'm going for a tried-and-true approach this time," Jessica insisted. "It turns out I just happen to have a wonderful knack with kids, especially spoiled-rotten six-year-olds. Taryn Bennet seems to be crazy about me."

"Really?" Lila was astonished.

"Really. I started telling her these silly stories the other day—sort of the kind my dad used to tell Liz and me—and she just ate them up! She begs me to tell her more whenever I'm around."

"So how's that going to convince Liz to switch jobs?"

"Well, all I have to do is keep it up and let Liz see how much Taryn needs me." Jessica smiled. "Elizabeth may not be willing to change jobs on *my* account, but she's far too sensitive to let a poor little girl suffer. See what I mean?"

Lila nodded admiringly. "You could even get Taryn to promote you all the time," she suggested. "Tell her to beg Liz for stories and then say they're not as good as yours. Really lay it on thick."

"Trust me," Jessica said sagely. "By the Fourth

of July I'll be at the Bennets' for the rest of the summer, and Elizabeth will be here."

From the confident look on Jessica's face, Lila had a feeling the discussion was closed. Jessica Wakefield was one of the cleverest girls she had ever met. If anyone could get her way in a situation like this, it was Jessica!

"Ben?" Lila called nervously in a low voice. It was darker on the beach than she had expected, and all she could hear was the whisper of the waves on the shore. Then she saw a shape emerge from the shadows. Her heartbeat quickened.

"Here I am," Ben called cheerfully. "I'm so glad you're here," he added, slipping an arm around her and pulling her close. Lila's head swam.

"Ben, let's talk," she said suddenly, pulling away from him slightly.

"What about?" he asked. "This is too pretty a night for *talking*."

Lila shivered. The breeze off the ocean was strong, and she wished she had brought a jacket. "I don't really know very much about you," she said hesitantly, feeling shy but wanting to find out something tangible about her mystery man. "Do you go to college up in San Francisco?"

"No," he said tersely.

From the tone of his voice, Lila could tell he wanted to change the subject, but she pressed him anyway, her curiosity roused. "Well, what do you do then? Do you have a job?"

Ben hesitated, then said, "I'm still in school." He was obviously embarrassed.

"School? You mean *high* school?" Lila's eyes widened in surprise and disappointment. Oh, well, she thought quickly, it wasn't the end of the world. He still seemed very adult. Maybe he'd been held back a year or two and was really eighteen or nineteen. "You don't have to sound so worried," she teased him. "I'm in high school, too. I just finished my junior year."

Ben put his arms around her again. "Let's get down to more important matters."

Lila giggled and held him away. "Not till you tell me what year you're in," she challenged. To her dismay, Ben's hands dropped from her shoulders, and he took a step back from her, his shoulders slumping dejectedly.

"I knew you'd find out," he said unhappily. "I thought you would when you asked me to take you to the movies. I thought you'd guess I didn't want to go because—"

"Because why?"

"Because I can't drive," Ben said. "I'm not old enough."

"Not *old* enough?" Lila stared at him, horror-stricken. "What—what are you trying to say, Ben?"

"I'm just going into my junior year." Ben sighed. 'See, I've always looked and acted a lot older than my age. But I won't be sixteen until September. I skipped a year because I went to a progressive private school, so—"

"You're only fifteen?" Lila was astonished. "Why didn't you tell me that from the beginning?"

"Now, wait a minute," Ben said angrily. "You didn't ask me. I haven't lied to you, Lila. The truth is I'm not ashamed of being younger than you. I was just afraid you'd react this way—and I'm disappointed because I really like you. I think we could have a great time together, if you'd just loosen up about something that doesn't even really matter!"

Lila felt the color draining from her cheeks. "Maybe you're right," she whispered. "I guess it really doesn't make that much difference. . . ." Her voice trailed off uncertainly.

Ben's face lit up. "I knew you were special." He gave her a big hug. "I knew I could count on you."

Lila didn't say anything for a minute. She did like Ben, and it seemed crazy to break things off just because of his age. But what about Jessica? If only she hadn't been so vocal about her romantic ideals, and especially about how immature high-school boys were. Jessica was sure to give her a hard time about that now. In fact, Jessica would probably never let her hear the end of it.

Unless . . .

"Ben," Lila said suddenly, facing him squarely, "what would you say if I were to ask you an enormous favor?"

"Your request is my command," Ben said with a mock bow.

"My friends are kind of peculiar about things like a guy's age," Lila said apologetically. "I'd like you to come to a party with me tomorrow night, but my best friend, Jessica, is going to be there, and she'd die if she found out how old you are. Would you mind pretending to be eighteen or nineteen, just in front of Jessica?"

"What party is this?" Ben was amused.

"A guy named Cliff Sherman is giving it. Why do you ask?"

"Well, let's put it this way." Ben pushed a lock of Lila's glossy hair back from her forehead. "I happen to be the guest of honor at that party. Cliff is one of my best friends. We went to summer camp together when we were kids, and I'm staying at his house for the next couple of weeks. I *don't* think I'll get very far pretending to be four years older than I am at *his* party!"

Lila's hopes were dashed. Wouldn't you know? She'd finally met a wonderful guy, and she couldn't even flaunt him in front of her friends. Jessica would never let her live it down when she found out Mr. Suave and Sophisticated was young enough to be her kid brother.

Unless Lila could cook up something fantastic in the next twenty-four hours, it looked as though Jessica would discover her secret at Cliff Sherman's party!

Nine

It was seven-thirty on Saturday night, and Elizabeth was getting her things together for her evening over at the Sargents' house. She slipped into her navy-blue cardigan. A quick glance in the mirror proved that she looked nice. Her skin was a soft rosy brown from the sun, and the white cotton shirt and skirt really brought out her tan.

Briefly she wondered what the party at Cliff's that night would be like. But she was glad to help Jessica out and actually looked forward to a quiet evening. She was upset about the way Jessica's job had turned out, and while Elizabeth had no intention of trading jobs, she did feel sorry for her twin. At least by sitting for Sam that night she could help a little.

"I hope you have a nice time tonight," Elizabeth said politely to Audrey Bennet, who was brushing Taryn's hair when Elizabeth stopped by the girl's bedroom to say good night.

Audrey looked beautiful, as always. Her hair was swept back in a chignon, and her black, off-the-shoulder dress made her look even taller and slimmer than usual. "I'm sure we will," she said pleasantly. "I hope you don't get too bored over at the Sargents'—not much of a night off for you, is it?"

Elizabeth smiled and shrugged. "I don't mind," she said. She looked wistfully at Taryn's face reflected in the mirror across the room. The girl looked so unhappy! As always, Elizabeth found herself wishing she could reach out to Taryn somehow, let her know she was on her side.

"Have fun, Taryn," she said lamely.

To her surprise, Taryn promptly burst into tears. "I don't want to go tonight. Momma, I don't want to go!"

Mrs. Bennet patted her shoulder awkwardly, smiling with obvious embarrassment at Elizabeth. "She's just a little tired," she said by way of explanation.

Elizabeth said good night to both of them, then stepped out into the hallway. What a sad little girl. If only . . .

She almost walked right into Malcolm Bennet,

who was coming toward her with a drink in his hand and a funny expression on his face. "Aren't they ready yet?" he exclaimed. "For goodness' sake, Audrey spends enough time dressing herself without getting Taryn started with the same self-absorption!"

Elizabeth didn't know what to say. "Excuse me," she managed to choke out, slipping past Mr. Bennet. She couldn't believe the way Malcolm talked about Audrey. It was awful that a husband and wife should treat each other as coldly as those two did!

Since Jessica had the Fiat, Josh Sargent picked Elizabeth up. She found it a relief to spend an evening in the Sargents' home. Despite the cramped, cluttered state of the little house, Lucy and Josh managed to fill the place with warmth and friendliness. Jessica had already left for Cliff's party with Lila, and Lucy was getting ready to leave herself.

"You're such a doll to come over tonight. I don't know what we could've done without you. It seemed such a shame to disappoint Jessica when she had her heart set on going to Cliff's," Lucy said warmly.

"I'm happy to be here," Elizabeth assured her.

Lucy wrote down the number where she and Josh could be reached in case of an emergency and took Elizabeth from room to room, pointing out everything she might need.

"Last but not least, the refrigerator," she said with a smile. "Help yourself to the chocolate cake and anything else that looks good. We should be home around midnight."

"Did you tell Liz about Jamie?" Josh asked from where he stood in the doorway, adjusting his tie.

"I thought you told her!" Lucy clapped a hand to her forehead. Lucy turned to Elizabeth. "An old family friend is coming to stay with us, only it turns out he's getting here a day sooner than we expected—which means tonight. His name's Jamie Galbraith, and he's really nice. He's twenty-one, and could you just let him in and tell him to make himself at home? He can put his things in the guest room off the porch."

Elizabeth nodded. "Sure," she said. She was a little disappointed that the quiet evening of reading and writing letters she had planned would be interrupted by conversation with a stranger. But she quickly forgot her apprehension in the flurry of goodbyes. Josh and Lucy finally pulled away from the curb in their Toyota. Sam was sound asleep, and the little house was perfectly still. Curling up in an armchair, Elizabeth picked up her novel. She was so absorbed by her reading that when the door bell rang half an hour later, she almost jumped out of her skin.

It wasn't until Elizabeth opened the front door that she remembered Jamie Galbraith. "Hello," she said to the dark-haired boy standing on the porch next to a canvas duffel bag. "Are you—?"

"Jamie," he said, smiling at her. He looked very collegiate, Elizabeth thought. His hair was fairly short, and he wore wire-rim glasses. A navy blue cotton polo shirt, faded khaki trousers, and scuffed topsiders completed the look.

"Come on in," Elizabeth said. She introduced herself, explaining she was filling in that night for her twin sister. "Lucy and Josh said you could leave your things here," Elizabeth said, smiling to herself as she flicked on the guest-room light switch. The Sargents' guest room was half the size of Taryn Bennet's closet!

"Lucy and Josh are great people," Jamie said enthusiastically, throwing his duffel bag down in the corner. "I don't know what I would've done this weekend if it weren't for them. I didn't plan to be in Malibu at all. It was kind of a last-minute decision, and I didn't have any other place to stay."

"Where are you from?" Elizabeth asked. She thought Jamie was pretty cute—too old for her but definitely cute.

"I'm from New York, but I'm going to school in Connecticut. I'm a junior at Yale." He had followed her back to the living room, and now they both sat down on the couch.

"Wow. Isn't Yale really hard?" Elizabeth was impressed. "What are you studying?"

"English," Jamie replied. "It *is* pretty tough," he added, "but I usually forget about that during the summer."

Elizabeth's eyes shone. "English is my favorite subject," she said passionately. "I want to be an English major at college, too."

"Really? Who's your favorite writer?" Jamie really looked interested.

"I keep changing my mind," Elizabeth confessed. "But I love to read." She showed him the novel she was in the middle of, and was fascinated to discover that he'd actually met the author. She couldn't get over how intelligent and attractive Jamie was. She went into the kitchen for some chocolate cake, and soon the two were talking like old friends.

"Let's listen to some music," Jamie suggested when they had polished off the last delicious crumbs. "Do you like jazz?" He was flipping through the Sargents' albums.

Elizabeth looked at him admiringly. "I really don't know very much about music," she admitted. "Do you?"

"A little," Jamie said, his back to her. "Here's a great album, Nina Simone." Soon the soft swells of music filled the room. "May I have this dance?" Jamie asked lightly.

Elizabeth blushed. "Oh—"

"Please," he said, suddenly serious.

Elizabeth smiled. "Why not?" she said softly,

stepping forward as he held out his arms. Up close he smelled like Ivory soap. She closed her eyes as he put his arms around her. It was so nice, dancing this way. . . . Elizabeth couldn't remember the last time she had slow danced. It seemed like forever. She had dated one boy, Todd Wilkins, for a long time, and after Todd moved to Vermont they had tried to hold on to their relationship, but it hadn't worked out. There hadn't been anyone since Todd who Elizabeth really cared about.

Until that night.

"Hey," Jamie said softly, putting his hand under her chin and tipping it up so he could look into her eyes. "You're really sweet, you know that?"

Elizabeth swallowed, her mouth dry. She had to remind herself that Jamie was twenty-one, older than her brother Steven, and way too old for her.

Then why was her heart hammering like crazy?

Suddenly Elizabeth broke away from Jamie's arms. "I think I hear Sam," she said, turning to hurry out of the room.

She was scared by the intensity of her reaction to the look in Jamie's eyes. *It just figures*, she thought as she bent over Sam's crib, *that the first special guy I've met in so long is too old for me*.

Sam was sound asleep, breathing softly and

evenly. Elizabeth adjusted his light blanket, kissed the top of his sweet-smelling head, and walked out of the room, partially closing the door behind her.

"Hey," Jamie said in a low voice when she returned. "I think I scared you, Liz. Am I right?"

Elizabeth cleared her throat. "I just feel kind of funny about this," she explained. "I mean, the Sargents aren't home and everything. And I'm—"

"You're the nicest girl I've talked to in a long, long time," Jamie said seriously. "You know, I meet a lot of girls at school—too many. Most of them think they're really hot stuff. They come on pretty strong. I can't remember the last time I met someone like you, someone soft and gentle. . . ."

Elizabeth's heart fluttered nervously. "I'm really young, though," she whispered. "I'm only sixteen, Jamie. Don't you think—"

"Look, you're right," Jamie said suddenly. "This really isn't the time for us to get to know each other better. For one thing, I'm really exhausted. I just drove all the way up from San Diego, and I'm probably not making much sense. Besides, you're here tonight to take care of little Sam. What do you say you and I get together sometime soon so we can really talk?"

Elizabeth blushed. Was he asking her for a

date? Sixteen must seem a little young to a junior in college.

"I don't know. I really don't—"

"Please," Jamie said firmly. "I don't know anyone around here, Liz, and I'd really like to spend some more time with you."

Elizabeth didn't know what to say. She knew her parents would never let her go out with someone Jamie's age if she were at home right now.

But her mother had asked her to use her own judgment this summer. When they came up to visit, she thought, she could broach the subject with them then—if she was even going out with him—but in the meantime Jamie seemed perfectly nice. In fact, *more* than perfectly nice. There couldn't possibly be any harm in getting together for a soda or something.

"Well, I have the day off on Monday—" Elizabeth began.

"Perfect!" Jamie exclaimed. "There's a place Josh and Lucy told me about right on the water, the Beach Café. We could meet there in the afternoon for coffee and a sandwich or something. How does that sound?"

Elizabeth grinned. "It sounds great," she said. No doubt about it, the idea of seeing Jamie Galbraith again was *very* appealing.

Who would have guessed an evening of baby-sitting would turn out to be so memorable?

Ten

"Isn't this fantastic?" Jessica's eyes sparkled with happiness as she surveyed the party around her.

"It's OK," Lila said flatly. She dreaded the moment when Ben would notice them. He would come over and start talking to her—and Jessica would find out her date was a fifteen-year-old.

Jessica pulled her blond hair over to one side. "Do I look all right?" she hissed, oblivious to the tortured look on Lila's face, since she had only one thing on her mind—making the right impression on her host.

"Yes," Lila said shortly. "You look as good as you looked the last ten times you looked in the mirror."

"My, my, my, aren't we in a bad mood tonight," Jessica said airily. "What's wrong with you, Li? I thought love was supposed to make you rosy-cheeked and charming, not a candidate for the Wicked Witch of the West's replacement."

Lila shrugged. "Maybe love affects different people in different ways."

Jessica giggled. "Well, it seems to be making you awfully grouchy, that's all I can say. Hey," she added, lowering her voice, "there's Cliff!"

Sure enough, Cliff was approaching them. Jessica thought he looked fabulous in a crisp white shirt and khaki trousers, very cool and summery. His bronzed face broke into a wide grin. "Jessica! Lila! I'm so glad you could make it! What do you think?" He waved a hand around him.

"It all looks wonderful," Jessica said sincerely. The beach behind the Shermans' house had been transformed. A portable dance floor blanketed the sand, and a live band played the latest rock music. Tiny twinkling lights strung from pole to pole around the dance floor illuminated tables covered with snowy linen cloths and heaped with desserts and soft drinks. About thirty people were milling around, chatting and dancing. And behind all this was the spectacular backdrop of the Pacific, the waves rolling gently up onto the beach. A luminous moon gleamed over the water. Jessica felt a shiver run up her spine. It was all so romantic!

"Have you two met my friend Ben yet?" Cliff looked searchingly around the crowd. "He's the guest of honor tonight. I'd really like you all to meet."

To Jessica's surprise Lila blushed. A good-looking boy with auburn hair was coming toward them, a drink in his hand. He looked vaguely familiar, but Jessica couldn't quite place him.

"Here he is now!" Cliff said. "Hey, Ben, come on over here. You've got to meet Malibu's two prettiest newcomers. Jessica, this is Ben Horgan. Ben, Jessica Wakefield."

"Hello," Jessica said, smiling. Where had she seen him before? she wondered.

"And this is Lila Fowler," Cliff continued.

Lila, still beet red, stared helplessly at Ben.

"Lila and I are old friends, aren't we?" Ben said, smiling straight at her. There seemed to be a question in his voice.

"Yes." Lila gulped. "Jessica, Ben is the guy I've been telling you about."

Jessica's eyes widened. So Lila's mystery man was Cliff's best friend from San Francisco! She'd seen Lila talking to him outside the dress shop in the Palm Mall. No wonder he looked familiar. The next instant Jessica realized why Lila was acting so funny. Hadn't Cliff mentioned to her that his friend was younger than he was? She couldn't wait to get Lila alone to find out.

But at the moment she had more important things on her mind. The band played the opening notes of the brand-new Tony Sargent song, "Tonight Is for You, Girl," and Cliff, a special smile on his face, was asking her to dance.

"You're a good dancer," Jessica murmured, looking up into Cliff's bright eyes as they swayed together.

"Not as good as you are. Have I told you how fantastic you look tonight?" Cliff said softly.

Jessica shook her head, her blond hair tumbling over her shoulders. "No," she said, her eyes intent on his, "you haven't."

"I think there's a lot you and I haven't said to each other yet." Cliff pulled her nearer as the music slowed. Jessica could feel his heart beating; her own was racing. She closed her eyes, thinking, *This is all too good to be true.*

It was a perfect evening. She could hear the surf crashing behind them, a gentle backdrop to the band's rendition of Tony Sargent's love lyrics. "All my life, girl, I've been living for now. Now it's comin' true girl, I'm telling you how . . ."

Jessica felt that the song had been written especially for her and for that evening. She took a deep breath as Cliff's arms tightened around her. Something told her this was going to be a wonderful summer after all.

"What's the story with you and Ben?" Jessica and Lila were in the Shermans' powder room, combing their hair and fixing their makeup.

Lila flushed. "Don't tease me about it," she said, her voice abrupt. "What difference does a guy's age make if you really like him?"

Jessica raised her eyebrows. "How old *is* Ben, Lila? Sixteen?"

Lila raked her brush furiously through her silky hair. "It doesn't matter how old he is," she snapped. "I told you, Jess, I don't want you bugging me about it."

"Who's the one who kept going on and on about meeting an older guy?" Jessica reminded her. "Who kept saying that high-school boys are babies?"

"Ben is different. He's—very mature for his age!"

Jessica could barely suppress her amusement. "I'm sure he is," she said consolingly. "Don't worry about it, Lila. You're little secret is safe with me."

Lila was furious. She knew Jessica's approach to keeping a secret was more like a full-fledged advertising campaign. "You'd better keep quiet about it, Jess, or I'll—"

"What?" Jessica said, mercilessly sweet. "Get Ben to sic his big brother on me?"

Lila shook her hairbrush at Jessica. "You don't know anything about love," she said. "It just so happens that when you care for someone, you can overlook small differences."

"Really?" Jessica was carefully lining her eyes with gray pencil. "Is that why you've been lecturing me for the past couple of months about wasting my time with high-school boys?"

Lila stuck her nose in the air. "You're too juvenile for words," she declared, sweeping her makeup back into its case and storming out of the powder room.

Jessica couldn't help being amused by Lila's predicament. It wasn't that she wanted to torment her friend. It was just she had gotten sick and tired of Lila's pretentious attitude about older men. This *was* the perfect time to give her back a little of her own medicine!

Back on the dance floor, Jessica dug for a little extra ammunition. "How old is your friend Ben?" she asked Cliff, taking a tiny sip of diet Coke.

Cliff laughed. "Are you checking up on him for Lila?"

Jessica pretended to look shocked. "Of course not," she said sweetly. "I'm just curious. He looks about seventeen."

"Well, actually, he's only fifteen," Cliff said.

"He's a year behind me in school, and I think he skipped a grade at some point. He's just a kid."

Jessica could barely contain her glee. It would have been bad enough if Lila had fallen in love with a guy their own age. But someone even younger than they were!

There was no doubt in Jessica's mind that her friend deserved her share of teasing about this uncharacteristic attachment. And she'd make sure to start teasing right away.

Jessica got back to the Sargents' at twelve-thirty. The Toyota wasn't in the drive. Josh and Lucy were still out, but that was fine with her. She couldn't wait to tell Elizabeth all about Cliff's party.

Jessica let herself in with her key. "It's only me!" she called softly as Elizabeth came out to the front hall. "Liz, thanks so much for sitting for me tonight! I had the most wonderful time."

"I had a nice time here, too," Elizabeth said nonchalantly as they walked into the living room.

"Whose stuff is that?" Jessica demanded, pointing at the knapsack and jacket Jamie had left on a chair before he'd excused himself, saying he was too tired to stay up a minute longer.

"Oh, the Sargents have a friend from the East

Coast staying here. He just arrived tonight,"
Elizabeth told her.

Jessica looked surprised. "A friend from the
East Coast? I wonder why they didn't mention
that to me."

Elizabeth shrugged. "Josh made it sound like
it was sort of a sudden thing. I guess Jamie was
in San Diego and just decided to come up here at
the last minute."

Jessica looked closely at her twin. "What's he
like?" She grimaced. "That's all we need—
another person staying in this tiny house!"

Elizabeth was quiet. She wished she could tell
Jessica what had happened that night. It had
been so long since anyone had made her feel the
way Jamie had. But part of her felt she should
keep her new friendship a secret. She knew it
was wrong for her to meet Jamie on Monday.
Her parents would be upset if they found out. It
wasn't fair to tell Jessica. It would force her to be
part of Elizabeth's deception. No, better to keep
the whole thing to herself.

"He's nice," Elizabeth said matter-of-factly.
"He's a junior at Yale—dark-haired, wire-rim
glasses, kind of cute in a preppy, intellectual sort
of way. He seems sort of shy."

Jessica rolled her eyes. "He'll probably have
his nose in a book the whole time."

Elizabeth smiled. "He seemed really nice to

106

me. Anyway, he was tired. He went to bed early."

"Where's he sleeping?"

"In the guest room."

Jessica snorted. "It figures. I would've been so much happier staying there. Do you have any idea what it's like, sleeping with a three-month-old baby inches away from you? No offense to Sam, but he makes the weirdest noises."

"Tell me about tonight," Elizabeth said, hoping to change the subject. She couldn't have asked a better question.

"It was the best party I've ever been to," Jessica declared dreamily, twirling around so the full skirt of her dress swirled around her. "Liz, I think I'm in love!"

Elizabeth grinned. "That's a surprise," she said dryly. "I don't suppose the lucky man happens to be Cliff Sherman?"

"How'd you guess?" Jessica giggled. "Oh, Liz, he's fantastic. He's so nice, so considerate. We danced for *hours*. We had such a good time. I have a feeling we're going to be seeing an awful lot of each other."

"Did Lila have fun?"

"You wouldn't believe it." Jessica sat down and planted her elbows on her knees, gleefully launching into a full account of what had transpired between Lila and Ben. "Can you *believe* it?

After all the nonsense she's given us about finding an older man!"

Elizabeth furrowed her eyebrows. "Well, it's nice that she's happy," she said firmly.

Jessica waved a hand impatiently. "I don't think we can let her get away with it. The way she's been talking lately, you'd think even saying *hello* to any guy under eighteen could ruin your reputation."

Elizabeth fiddled with the cover of her novel. "Well, I'm sure she's embarrassed enough about it as it is, Jess."

Jessica laughed. "Not possible! I for one intend to embarrass her further. By the way, Liz, you have to come wind surfing with us on Monday. Ben and Lila and Cliff and some friend of theirs named Brent are all going. Cliff says Brent's cute. I told him I'd ask you if you wanted to get fixed up with him."

Elizabeth thought quickly. "I don't think so, Jess. I promised Taryn I'd take her somewhere special Monday afternoon."

"On your day off? That's crazy! If you don't have any fun this summer, you'll go insane."

Elizabeth hated lying to Jessica, but she didn't feel she had a choice. "I don't mind," she insisted. "I really want Taryn to like me. Anyway, it's only one afternoon. We still have the whole summer."

Jessica was disappointed. "Please come," she

begged. "I really want to fix you up with this guy Brent. It isn't fair, Liz. I have Cliff, and Lila has Ben. It isn't fair for you to be stuck with *Taryn* on your day off!"

"It's not as bad as it seems." Elizabeth didn't sound very convincing, even to herself. "I'll meet somebody one of these days. Don't worry about it, Jess."

Jessica still looked pained. "Will you at least think it over? I told Cliff I'd call him tomorrow and let him know."

Elizabeth sat straighter on the couch. She could hear the Toyota pulling up in the drive. Josh and Lucy were back.

"Honestly, Jess, I just can't make it this time," she said, forcing her voice to be steady and firm.

Elizabeth realized that getting together with Jamie was even more complicated than she had first anticipated. She hated lying to her sister. She knew now what she was doing was wrong—really wrong. She was going to have to let Jamie know on Monday that she wouldn't be able to see him again.

Eleven

"This place is wonderful," Elizabeth said appreciatively, taking a sip of the delicious Italian citrus drink she had ordered. The Beach Café was a small, brilliant-white restaurant at the end of a pier, hanging right over the sparkling blue Pacific. It was very small, only six or seven tables, and this late in the afternoon it was practically empty. The perfect place for a secret date.

"This place isn't all that's wonderful," Jamie said, putting his hands over Elizabeth's and staring deep into her eyes.

Elizabeth cleared her throat nervously and pulled back her hands. "Um, how did you find out about it? I thought you didn't know Malibu very well."

Jamie shrugged and smiled mysteriously.

"Can't a guy have any secrets around you, Elizabeth Wakefield?" She continued looking at him expectantly until he relented. "Josh told me about it. He and Lucy know everything there is to know about Malibu."

"You haven't seen them in a long time, have you?" Elizabeth asked.

Jamie cocked his head. "I feel like I'm being interviewed," he said lightly. "You wouldn't happen to be checking up on my history, would you?"

Elizabeth colored slightly. "I feel like I don't know very much about you," she admitted. There was something different about Jamie, though she couldn't quite put her finger on it. She had no reason to doubt anything he'd told her about himself. She was probably just acting paranoid because she felt guilty for sneaking out to meet him.

"Well, there isn't much to know about my past," Jamie said seriously, taking her hand again. "I'm from an absolutely normal, all-American family in New York. My dad's a doctor, my mom's a housewife. No brothers, no sisters, no pets—nothing out of the ordinary except a little loneliness."

Elizabeth smiled warmly at him. "I hope you don't hate me for being curious about you. I feel like I've told you so much about myself, about my family and Jessica and everything. I can't help wondering about—well, you know. Just about everything."

"I'll tell you this much," Jamie said, gripping her hand tightly. "I feel like a whole new part of my life got started when I opened the Sargents' door on Saturday night and saw you looking out at me."

Elizabeth dropped her eyes. "Jamie, I—"

"Don't say it," he pleaded. "Liz, I know what you're thinking. You're worrying about the difference in our ages, right?"

Elizabeth sighed. "Twenty-one is pretty old, Jamie. My parents would never approve. I know this is going to sound weird to you, but I feel terrible doing something I know they'd consider wrong."

"That doesn't sound weird. It sounds honest," Jamie told her. "But I can't stand the thought of not seeing you, Liz. You're the best thing that's happened to me in a long time."

Elizabeth was quiet for a minute. "I like you, too—a lot," she said sincerely. "But it seems like we're only setting ourselves up for a fall. There's no way anything could ever come of this, Jamie. If we keep seeing each other, it'll have to be with the understanding that it's just—for now. Do you know what I mean?"

Jamie looked at her thoughtfully. "I guess I do," he said. "I don't know if you can control life that way, but I see what you're trying to say."

"And another thing," Elizabeth said with feeling, "we'll have to keep it quiet, Jamie. If Jessica finds out—"

"Aw, Jessica seems like a good sport. I can't imagine that she wouldn't support whatever you did."

Elizabeth shook her head. "I don't want her to know about us, Jamie. I'm not kidding. It would put her in an unfair position. Until my parents come to see us and I have a chance to talk to them in person. . . ." Her voice trailed off, but her eyes begged him to understand.

"All right," Jamie conceded. "Look, Liz, as far as I'm concerned, I just want to see you, be with you. I'm willing to agree to any terms you set up."

"Well," Elizabeth said, taking a deep breath, "I know this really isn't meant to be, but I can't help feeling . . . I don't know, I guess I just want to be with you, too."

Jamie squeezed her hand tightly. She really was a special girl. He wished there was some way to explain everything to her—from the very beginning. It was funny. He'd come to Malibu to make sure no one would find him. Above all he wanted to keep his identity a secret.

And now he had met someone he could really care about. Someone to whom he would like to tell the truth. But he couldn't. There was too much at stake.

*   *   *

It was crazy, he thought, looking over the water as he waited for Elizabeth to finish making a phone call to the Bennets' house. He had experienced a lot of things so far in his life, but he had never imagined assuming a disguise as a "regular" guy could be so exhilarating. He had figured the couple of weeks he'd have to spend in Malibu with his cousin would be incredibly boring. He hadn't counted on meeting Elizabeth.

Tony Sargent had never lived an ordinary life—not since he was a kid. When he was eleven he had won a singing contest, and he was given the chance to sing with a band on a radio station.

That ended Tony Sargent's normal life. All of a sudden people were calling his parents, telling them their son was real star material. By the time he was thirteen, Tony had a manager and was singing at clubs in Los Angeles. Teen magazines plastered his picture all over their covers, and fan mail started pouring in. That was only the beginning. Tony's manager, Jody Philips, was sharp. He knew the market, and he knew he had a star in Tony Sargent. Soon Tony was appearing on TV talk shows. Next, he recorded his first album, and one of his songs made it to number one. Then he had gotten a movie contract.

Tony Sargent was a star.

Sometimes he couldn't believe it had all happened so fast. He was only seventeen, and already he had things some people never had, such as fame and a lot of money. But he didn't have what other guys his age took for granted—the chance to just hang out, relax with friends, have a good time.

He was always on the run. He had left school at fourteen, studying with private tutors after that, and it was beginning to look as though college would be pretty hard to swing. He would have loved attending Yale, to study English the way "Jamie Galbraith" did. It was funny. He came to Malibu to save his life, and what he found was that his "disguise" was more than that: It was a chance to become someone he had always secretly wanted to be. He just hoped Elizabeth never found out the truth.

Tony's trouble started the year before. He had been on the road for several months and was tired and lonely. It was summer, and he found himself really missing his parents and his home in New York. Maybe that was why he'd gotten involved with Lisa.

She was exactly the kind of girl he'd always stayed away from—a groupie, not a real friend. She approached Tony after a concert, and in a moment of weakness he agreed to have a drink with her. She seemed like a nice girl, but it turned out she was mixed up with a bad crowd.

116

That drink was one of the stupidest things he ever did.

It turned out Lisa had a boyfriend—a jealous boyfriend. A boyfriend who was in jail for assault and battery. None of this got back to Tony until months after he returned to L.A. He started getting threatening letters and phone calls. The police were convinced they were from Lisa's boyfriend, Frankie LaSalle, who had gotten out of jail, but so far they hadn't tracked him down.

Meanwhile, Tony's agent convinced him to do something drastic. With his blond hair and famous blue eyes, Tony was recognized wherever he went. He was a household name—a great advantage when it came to his career but a real drawback now that he was being hunted by a crackpot.

Jody came up with the idea of Malibu. Josh and Lucy's place was perfect—an average house in a nondescript part of town. No one would look for him there. Jody hired the best makeup men in Los Angeles to help Tony with his disguise. His hair was dyed brown and cut short. Dark-tinted contact lenses and wire-rim glasses toned down his eyes and made him look more intellectual.

So he had come to Malibu as Jamie Galbraith. The only people who knew where he was were his agent and his private secretary, Julie. It was all drastic, but the letters and phone calls made one thing clear: Frankie meant business. He wanted to kill Tony for messing around with his girlfriend.

Tony felt amazingly safe in his disguise. He liked his cousin Josh, and Lucy and little Sam were great, too. Hiding out was more fun than he'd ever imagined. Elizabeth's sister Jessica was high-spirited and funny, and he loved teasing her.

Best of all, there was Elizabeth.

He couldn't believe what fun it was to be with a girl who thought he was special because of what he was rather than who he was. Ordinarily, it was so hard for him to meet anyone. People either freaked out when they discovered he was a star or made a ridiculous fuss.

But Elizabeth . . . she liked *him*. She wanted to know what he thought about things—about literature, about people. She admired him for his own sake. He couldn't believe what a nice feeling that was.

And he admired her, too. He had dreamed of meeting someone as frank and down-to-earth and beautiful as Elizabeth. He just hoped they could keep seeing each other. He didn't know how much longer he would stay in Malibu. And he was sure if Elizabeth ever found out who he really was, she wouldn't want to have anything to do with him.

He would just have to treasure every minute they had together and try to find some way to make this magical summer escape last and last!

"Hey, how did you get so good at wind surfing?" Jessica demanded, pushing her wet hair back. She was completely sopping and completely out of breath.

"I took lessons last summer," Lila whispered. "But don't tell Ben. He thinks I learned it all from him."

"Well," Jessica said, her eyes twinkling mischievously, "maybe you can teach him something in return. You could tutor him in biology or something. After all, you're so much older and wiser than he is!"

"Listen, Jess—" Lila began angrily.

"Hey, you two, are you coming out again or what?" Cliff called from where he stood, waist-deep in water.

"I've had it with your snotty wisecracks," Lila hissed. "I'm not kidding, Jess. You've got to cut it out."

"Don't you think you're being awfully defensive?" Jessica's voice was silky. "I'm *only* teasing."

"Well, I don't think it's funny. I happen to care about Ben a great deal," Lila said indignantly.

Jessica thought about this as she waved at Cliff

to let him know they were coming. "You'd better be careful," she warned her friend as they waded back into the water. "He's probably very vulnerable. You might even be his first girlfriend!"

Lila's eyes sparked. "Shut up," she whispered furiously. "I'm serious, Jess. I've had just about all I can take from you."

Lila was even angrier than Jessica guessed. But she was determined not to let her friend's behavior spoil her budding romance with Ben.

Twelve

"Just ignore him," Jessica advised Cliff softly.
The two were in the Sargents' living room,
stretched out on the carpet with a backgammon
board between them. Sam was in his playpen
nearby, and Jamie Galbraith was pacing up and
down, looking at his watch.

"I'll be back in a minute," he said finally, leaving the room without a glance in their direction.

"He seems like a weird guy," Cliff observed,
moving five of his pieces over to the next dia-
mond. "What's his story?"

Jessica shrugged. "He's definitely bizarre,"
she agreed. "I don't know what he's doing
here—other than driving me crazy! All he ever
does is read the paper or that dumb novel that's
about a million pages long. Or listen to really

strange music. I hope he goes soon," she added, throwing the dice.

Cliff patted her hand and smiled. "So you mean I shouldn't be jealous because you're sharing close quarters with an older, intellectual guy from Yale?"

Jessica's aqua eyes opened wide. "You've got to be kidding," she said, insulted. "How can you even suggest something as terrible as that? Don't you think I've got better taste?"

"I just hope," Cliff said, his voice low and husky, "that you keep thinking I'm worth wasting time with. That's all I care about."

Jessica's heart began to pound as he leaned toward her over the board. "Watch out!" His hand pushed down on the board, and game pieces skated all over. But she really didn't care, and she knew Cliff didn't either.

The next thing she knew, his lips were touching hers. She slipped her arms over his shoulders and around his neck, burying her fingers in his thick, soft hair. He smelled so nice, and his mouth was so warm . . .

Jamie cleared his throat when he came back into the room. Jessica nearly jumped out of her skin. "I hate to interrupt, but I just want to let you know I'm heading out," he said abruptly. "I've got an appointment in Santa Monica."

"OK," Jessica said huffily. *Good riddance!* she was thinking. Whoever this Jamie Galbraith guy was, he sure seemed creepy to her. She couldn't wait until he left the Sargents' house for good.

"Jamie, are you sure we should be meeting here?" Elizabeth bit her lip, fighting a pang of guilt. It had been so much trouble getting to Santa Monica. First, she had had to borrow a car from the Bennets—not that they'd really cared. She also had to get Maria's permission to leave the house that afternoon. Elizabeth knew she was doing something she shouldn't.

But the thought of seeing Jamie again made everything worthwhile. She was so full of her feelings for him she thought she would burst. The night before, she had come very close to confiding in Jessica. She and her sister always talked to each other about their new loves. But at the last minute Jessica had started saying what a creep Jamie was. All the things that made him special to Elizabeth struck her twin as completely weird.

This was something Elizabeth was just going to have to go through alone.

"We'll have a wonderful afternoon together— and a wonderful evening," Jamie assured her enthusiastically. Slinging an arm around her shoulders, he outlined his plans: first a walk on the beach, then a seafood dinner at one of the nicest places in town.

"That does sound fantastic." Elizabeth felt a thrill of anticipation. She couldn't get over how much she liked this guy. It had been so long. . . .

Jamie was right. It was the nicest evening she could remember. Everything was perfect. The bright, sunny day gave way to a clear, cool evening. They had plenty of time to window-shop in town and stroll along the beach before heading to the restaurant. The meal was fabulous, but Elizabeth almost forgot to eat in her fascination with Jamie.

She was falling in love with him. In spite of all her logical reservations, she was beginning to feel the only thing that mattered in the whole world was Jamie Galbraith.

They talked about everything—his love of music, his interest in books and literature, his travels. Now and then Elizabeth thought she detected something wistful in his words. No, she decided, it was only her imagination.

The most magical moment came just before they split up to drive back. They had parked their cars at the restaurant, and as Elizabeth reluctantly opened the door of the Bennets' black Camaro, Jamie slipped his arm through hers. "Come look at the moon first," he said, his voice low. Elizabeth followed him to a bench in the small clifftop garden overlooking the sea, adjacent to the restaurant. She could hardly believe the beauty of the scene before her, the waves washed with silver by the moon. Her throat ached as she stared out over the water. She was intensely aware of Jamie's body next to hers.

"Elizabeth," he said softly, lingering over the syllables of her name. He cupped her chin in his hand, tilting it so her wide eyes stared into his.

"Thank you for tonight," he whispered. The next thing she knew she was in his arms, kissing and holding him as if she might never let go.

"Have you noticed anything weird about Liz lately?" Jessica and Lila were on the beach, watching Taryn dart back and forth between the waves. Elizabeth was still up at the Bennets', having just called down to say she'd be with them in a minute.

"Not really. What do you mean?" Lila looked puzzled.

"Maybe I'm just hypersensitive," Jessica said, "but I keep feeling as if she's holding something back every time we speak."

Lila giggled. "You just feel guilty because you're trying so hard to scheme her out of her job."

"No, that isn't it," Jessica insisted. "Although I *am* still trying—I'll admit it! Taryn's getting to be a pain, though. She sticks to me like a burr."

"She isn't sticking to you now," Lila observed.

Jessica frowned. "Maybe I'd better redouble

my efforts. I've got a really good 'secret' to tell her this time." Getting to her feet with an effort, Jessica threw her head back, shaking out her bright, glossy hair. The sun felt so good on her face! she thought. But back to business—Taryn. She crossed the sand to crouch down beside the little girl.

"Hi, Taryn!" she sang out. "How're you?"

Taryn squinted up at her. "OK," she said, a tiny glimmer of a smile crossing her face.

Jessica scooped up a handful of white sand and ran it through her fingers. "Want me to tell you another secret?" she asked casually.

Taryn's eyes brightened. "Yes," she said seriously, staring at Jessica as if she were a magician.

"Good. This is a really special, special secret, but you have to promise to keep it quiet. OK?"

Taryn nodded vigorously.

"Once upon a time there was a wicked little girl named Taryn. She didn't know it, but she wasn't really a little girl at all. Do you know what she was?"

Taryn shook her head, bug-eyed.

"She was a beautiful princess," Jessica said dramatically. "But she was really in trouble because she was under a bad spell that made her wicked. Once the spell was broken, do you know what happened to that wicked little girl?"

"She got nice?" Taryn suggested, stuffing her thumb in her mouth.

"Yes!" Jessica shrieked, throwing her arms around the child.

Taryn chuckled joyfully. "I like that," she said shyly, taking her thumb out of her mouth. "I like *you*," she added, her blue eyes glowing.

Jessica patted her happily on the head. She felt like patting *herself* on the back. She couldn't have planned things better. *Congratulations, Jess!* she thought triumphantly. *You've won this impossible little girl over.*

And in no time she would make her sister realize that it was really much better for Taryn if the two of them swapped jobs for the rest of the summer!

Thirteen

"I don't care what you say." Audrey Bennet turned on her husband with anger flashing from her clear blue eyes. "I'm sick and tired of the way you've been acting, Malcolm! Either you cut it out or—"

"Or what?" Malcolm jeered, crossing his arms and glaring at his wife, who was sitting at her dressing table in the bedroom. "You always do this. You deliver ultimatums instead of carrying on a conversation. This past year has been hell for me, Audrey. Why do you think I spend all my time at the club? If you'd meet me halfway—"

Audrey felt tears welling up in her eyes. *I've got to control myself. I've got to show him I don't care what he says*, she thought. They were getting ready for a dinner party that neither was looking forward to. She didn't even remember now what had sparked the argument. It seemed that they were always arguing lately. Malcolm was tense and irritable, and she knew she wasn't exactly easygoing either. That night, though, she had really been ready for a truce. But here they went again. Malcolm was livid, and she was about to crumble.

"Pull yourself together," Malcolm said roughly. "Don't give me that stricken look, Audrey. I can't bear it."

"Sometimes I think you really hate me," Audrey whispered, the color draining from her cheeks. She didn't notice the bedroom door inching open. Taryn was coming down with a virus and should have been in bed. Now she stood frozen in the doorway, listening to the heated exchange between her parents, her blue eyes enormous.

"You only think of yourself." Malcolm raised his voice. "What about Taryn? You never think about her. You just leave her with Maria while you run around, spending money on clothes you never even wear."

Audrey flushed. "You're hardly an ideal father," she retorted. "When was the last time *you* were around to spend time with her?"

"You shouldn't have ever had a child," Malcolm said viciously. "You don't know the first thing about loving Taryn or loving anyone for that matter!''

Audrey stared at him, her lips quivering. "If you feel that way, if you think our entire marriage is a waste, I think I should leave." Her voice cracked.

"Don't bother." Malcolm grabbed his keys from the dresser. "Because I'm going to make it easy for you. *I'm* going to leave. You just sit there and watch me."

As he stormed out into the hallway, he didn't notice Taryn cowering nearby. A few moments later, the front door slammed, sending an echo of finality through the suddenly quiet house.

"Taryn, what's wrong?" Elizabeth asked, a worried frown darkening her pretty face. The little girl was in her bed, sobbing uncontrollably. She was flushed and warm; Elizabeth suspected a fever. "Has she had aspirin?" she asked Maria.

Maria shook her head. "She won't take any. She won't eat, either. She just keeps crying and crying. She won't tell me why."

"Let me talk to her alone. Maybe she'll tell me what's bothering her."

Neither Audrey nor Malcolm had been at home when Elizabeth returned from her rendezvous with Jamie at the Beach Café. Audrey had left a brief note saying they were at a dinner party and would be home late. "P.S.," the note read. "Please keep an eye on Taryn. I think she's coming down with something."

Elizabeth sighed. No wonder poor Taryn was such a monster. Imagine being nothing more than a postscript on a hastily scribbled note! She laid her hand on the child's head and frowned at how hot Taryn felt. "Taryn," she whispered. "It's me, Elizabeth. Can you tell me what's the matter? Are you upset because you feel sick, or is it something else?"

Taryn's eyes filled with tears. "Leave me alone," she whimpered. "I don't feel good."

"I won't leave you alone," Elizabeth said firmly. "I'm going to stay right here with you until you feel better. Do you understand?"

Taryn was silent, the long lashes of her closed eyes dark against her flushed, round cheeks.

"Now, I happen to think something is bugging you, and I want to know what it is," Elizabeth said conversationally, pulling a chair up beside the bed.

Taryn began to sob. "My daddy . . . my daddy hates my mommy," she said in a strangled voice.

Elizabeth stared at her. "Of course he doesn't!" she declared. "Where did you get that idea?"

"I heard them," Taryn said between sobs. "I heard them talking."

"Taryn, did you overhear your parents having an argument?"

Taryn nodded, tears spilling down her cheeks.

Elizabeth took a deep breath. "Were they very angry with each other?"

Taryn nodded again. "They said . . . they hated each other. They said they should never have had me!"

Elizabeth leaned forward to gather Taryn in her arms. "Listen," she said softly, rocking the child gently, "they couldn't possibly have meant that. Sometimes people get angry and say stupid things to each other. But, Taryn, your parents love you very much. There's no way they would ever be sorry that you were their little girl."

Taryn only kept crying.

"You just have to help them to realize how much they need each other," Elizabeth continued.

Taryn looked up, her eyes heartbreakingly sad. "I don't feel good," she whispered. "I want to sleep now."

Elizabeth sighed. Nothing she could do ever seemed to help. "I want you to take some aspirin first," she said, reaching for the tablets on Taryn's night table.

She watched Taryn dutifully chew the baby aspirin but still couldn't bring herself to leave her. "I'll tell you what," she said finally. "I'll sit in this armchair of yours until you fall asleep,

OK? That way if you feel like talking to me about what happened tonight I'll be here for you."

Taryn didn't answer. Every now and then Elizabeth heard a small, stifled sob, then finally the little girl was silent. Elizabeth crept silently from the room.

Taryn listened to her go. She couldn't sleep. Her chest hurt when she breathed, and she felt hot, then cold. She couldn't help hearing over and over the things her parents had said that evening. Her mom and dad didn't love her! That was why they spent hardly any time at home. Her parents didn't love her. They never had. For some reason she couldn't quite understand, the anger and hatred in the house was all her fault. It was because of her that they were arguing. Hadn't they said it would have been better if they'd never had her?

Well, Taryn thought, she wouldn't stay there anymore. She would run away.

The minute she was sure Elizabeth was safely out of earshot, Taryn slipped out of bed. She saw her way to her closet by the night-light and took out the small suitcase her mother always packed for her when they went to Palm Springs. She felt dizzy standing up, but she managed to drag the little bag over to her bureau. She packed her favorite doll, a sweater, and a pair of pajamas.

She was going to run away to her grandparents' house in Nebraska. She wasn't exactly sure where Nebraska was, but she'd get there some-how. Sliding her suitcase under her bed, she crawled back under the covers.

She could hardly wait for the next day. Wher-ever Nebraska was, Taryn was positive it had to be better than Malibu.

Fourteen

Elizabeth checked her reflection in the mirror. She wasn't sure about the new shirt she was wearing. It might be a little . . . well, a little too bare. She wished Jessica were there to consult with her. There had been so many times this summer when she'd really missed having her twin right down the hall.

Elizabeth flicked on the radio as she reached for her hairbrush. The sky outside her bedroom window at the Bennets' looked threatening, and she wanted to hear a weather report before going out. She was meeting Jamie at the Beach Café again.

Elizabeth checked her watch. It was three-thirty. She'd better get going, or she'd be late for Jamie. Her heartbeat quickened at the thought of seeing him, being with him in just half an hour. She couldn't get over the strength of her feelings for him. She wished she could enjoy this relationship without the worry and guilt. It would be such a relief to talk it over with her parents during their visit, and then be free to share her feelings with Jessica as well.

"Maria, I'll be back by six," she called, turning the radio off as she slipped out of her room into the hallway.

Maria emerged from Taryn's suite, obviously upset. Taryn had been in bed all day with a fever and a hacking cough. "She really feels hot to me. I hope that the cough medicine helps."

"When will Audrey and Malcolm be back?" Elizabeth asked.

Maria shook her head. "I don't know. I don't think they're together, actually. Malcolm's at the club, and I think Audrey is at her mother's."

Elizabeth wondered if Maria knew Malcolm hadn't been home the night before. It seemed like everything in the Bennet household was suddenly topsy-turvy. Elizabeth felt tense for some reason; the general atmosphere was tense.

"How are you getting to your friend's?"

"Well," Elizabeth said, "I was going to take the bus."

Maria shook her head. "Wait right here." She returned a few moments later with the keys to the Camaro, which she handed to Liz. "Take the

Camaro, Liz. I don't want you waiting for the bus in the pouring rain. That's all we need—for you to get sick, too."

"Well . . ." Elizabeth hesitated. She hated to borrow the car, but it did look bad outside. The sky was dark gray, and thick, purplish clouds were rolling in. "OK." She nodded thankfully. "I promise I'll be back soon."

Several minutes later Elizabeth was pulling the car out of the driveway. She turned onto the long street leading up toward the main road to town. A blur of static interrupted the song on the radio, and then the disc jockey broke in. "We interrupt this program to broadcast the following emergency announcement from the National Weather Service. A severe thunderstorm warning has been issued for all residents of Los Angeles County. A small-craft warning is in immediate effect. All small boats should seek shelter at once. We're expecting serious flooding and accompanying mudslides from the rains. Please try to stay off the roads."

Elizabeth squinted up at the sky. It really did look awful out, and now she could hear the low rumble of approaching thunder. A fork of heat lightning flashed over the distant mountains. For a minute she thought about turning back. But there was no way she was going to stand Jamie up.

"I'll be fine," she assured herself. The weather

service usually overstated things, just to make sure people were cautious. She was an excellent driver, and so far it wasn't even raining. These summer storms often blew over before they even hit, she reasoned.

Elizabeth made a right onto the coast road and put her foot on the gas, heading on toward the Beach Café.

Maria had enough to worry about between Taryn's illness and Elizabeth driving in this storm. Now she had to deal with Malcolm Bennet's ill humor. "No, she isn't here," Maria said into the phone, shifting her weight from one foot to the other uncomfortably. "No, Mr. Bennet. I haven't seen her all day, and she didn't leave a note."

Maria hated being caught between husband and wife like this. Audrey had specifically told her not to let Malcolm know where she was, and Maria could tell from his irritated tone that he suspected her of withholding just that information.

"Well, tell her I'm at the club," he said gruffly. "Wherever she is I only hope she isn't in her car. It looks like we're in for a bad storm, and Audrey isn't much use driving in the rain."

"I'll be sure to tell her, Mr. Bennet," Maria said.

Taryn opened the door to her suite a crack. Maria was on the phone—good! The path was clear. Clutching her little suitcase firmly in her hand, Taryn tiptoed down the stairs. She held her breath as she darted to the front door.

Maria didn't see her.

For a minute Taryn couldn't get the door open. It seemed to be stuck. She twisted the slippery knob with all her might, and at last it gave way. Large raindrops were spattering on the pavement as she half ran, half stumbled down the driveway, her suitcase bumping against her leg.

But Taryn didn't even notice the rain or the nagging pain in her chest when she breathed. As she hurried down the street, all she could think was that she was doing the right thing, what everyone wanted her to do. They would be much better off without her.

She kept on stumbling forward as the rain got heavier and heavier. She had promised herself one thing, and she was sticking to her promise.

She didn't look back once.

Jessica shivered as she stood on the Bennets' porch, hopping from one foot to the other. She shook her arms and head, and water flew in every direction. "Come on, already," she muttered, jabbing at the door bell again with her fist. She couldn't believe how hard it was raining.

She had barely been able to see the street when she was driving. She'd been out, and when she heard the flood warning on the radio, she had headed straight back to the Sargents', but at the last minute her sixth sense—it was part of being a twin—sent her to the Bennets' to check on Elizabeth. Cliff and his parents were in Los Angeles visiting relatives, so Jessica knew he was safe. But Elizabeth and the Bennets were so close to the ocean, and the biggest storm in years was heading straight toward them.

At last the front door opened, and Jessica hurried inside, embarrassed by the amount of water she brought in with her.

"We haven't met," she said to Maria. "I'm Elizabeth's twin sister. You must be Maria."

Maria tried to smile, but she was too worried. "It really is bad out there, isn't it? You're soaked, poor thing!"

"I'm all right," Jessica said. "I just wanted to make sure Elizabeth was safe. On the emergency broadcast a minute ago they were talking about maybe evacuating people from along the shore."

Maria's dark eyes filled with horror. "Liz isn't here," she said, her voice shaking. "She was going somewhere. She said she was meeting a friend."

Jessica vaguely wondered what friend Maria could mean. But she was too distressed to think of anything other than her twin's safety. "She really shouldn't be on the road now. But, well, maybe she's better off in town. Maria, I think we should get Taryn and get out of here. It's really dangerous to stay near the ocean in a storm this severe."

"I let Liz take my car," Maria said, extremely concerned.

"That's all right, I've got the Fiat," Jessica said. "Why don't you go round up Taryn?"

Maria hurried to the little girl's suite, and Jessica tried to dry herself off with a towel from the powder room. She couldn't believe how black it had gotten outside. She just hoped Elizabeth was somewhere inside—and somewhere safe!

A few minutes later, Maria came running back, her face white as a sheet. "Taryn isn't in her room," she cried, her lips trembling.

Jessica's heart skipped a beat. She stared at Maria. "What do you mean?"

Maria's eyes filled with tears. "She isn't anywhere! Her bed is empty. She must have slipped outside when I was on the phone!"

"But why would she do that?"

Maria was trembling violently. "She's been very upset. Mr. and Mrs. Bennet had a terrible fight last night, and Elizabeth said Taryn overheard something—"

"We'll have to go look for her," Jessica said quickly. "Maria, you call the police. I'm going to see if I can find some boots and raincoats." Maria dashed to the phone, and Jessica rummaged through the front-hall closet, extricating some galoshes and two old slickers. It occurred to her that it was funny to be putting on a raincoat when she was already soaked to the skin.

But not that funny. Jessica shivered. She didn't even want to think what kind of danger little Taryn could be in, wandering alone outside in the rapidly worsening weather.

She just knew that she and Maria would have to find her. They didn't have a minute to lose.

Lucy Sargent frowned when she heard the door bell ring. "Maybe that's Jessica," she said to herself, hurrying to the front door. With the rain really pounding down and the radio instructing everyone to stay indoors, Lucy was concerned about her baby-sitter.

To her surprise, a heavyset, dark-haired man was standing on the porch.

"Can I help you?" she asked.

"Yes." He put out his hand. "My name is Jody Philips. I'm Tony's manager."

"Oh!" Lucy said, surprised. "Come on in!"

"Thanks, but I'm in a real hurry," he told her. "I have to see Tony right away. I've got something to talk over with him that just can't wait. Can you tell me where I can find him?"

Lucy paled. "It isn't about that man, is it? The one he's hiding from?"

"Yes," he said, sighing heavily. "It is."

Lucy was frightened. "He's at a place called the Beach Café. You go down Route Nine and turn left down a little road called Breakwater Way. The restaurant is right at the end of the pier." She frowned, looking up at the stormy sky. "I'm worried about him. He shouldn't be out there!"

"I'll take care of him," he said gruffly. The next minute he was striding back through the pelting rain to his car.

"Who was that?" Josh called from the living room.

"Jody Philips, Tony's manager," Lucy said. She closed the door behind her and leaned back against it. She rubbed her forehead. Something was bothering her, but she couldn't put her finger on it.

"What did he want?" Josh joined her, looking worried.

"He wanted to talk to Tony. I told him where he was. Is that OK?"

Josh just looked at her. "Why shouldn't it be OK?" he asked. "Jody wouldn't hurt Tony. He's the one who's so concerned about his safety, remember?"

*   *   *

Frankie LaSalle squinted through the streams of water running down his windshield. He couldn't believe this weather. Just his luck to be looking for Tony Sargent in the worst storm to hit California in years.

On the other hand, he had been lucky so far—more than lucky.

First he had convinced that stupid secretary of Tony Sargent's that he had to get through to him. She tried saying she wasn't authorized to give out his address, but he wouldn't fall for that. "This is the police calling," he had said sternly. "We've just picked up his father in Connecticut. He's been in a serious car crash. Tony Sargent is named as his next of kin. We have to get him out here right away. His father is dying."

And she'd fallen for it. She hemmed and hawed but finally came out with the address of the place in Malibu where Tony was hiding out and had given him the name Tony was using. As if Tony really thought he could hide from Frankie LaSalle.

Frankie meant business. Lisa had told him all about Tony when she visited him in jail, and the minute he heard what had happened, Frankie made up his mind that he would get even with Tony as soon as he got out of jail. Whatever it took, Frankie would get back at him.

Now he had his chance. Tony was probably

stranded at the restaurant because of the storm. Frankie sure had pulled a fast one on that lady Tony was staying with. She'd believed he was Jody Philips! What a joke. Only it wouldn't be a laughing matter for long, Frankie was going to make sure of that. When he got to the Beach Café, he'd make sure *he* had the last laugh. Tony Sargent was never going to touch Lisa again—or any girl.

"Get ready, guy," he said grimly, gripping the steering wheel as he swerved onto Breakwater Way. "Tony Sargent, you're a dead man!"

His thick lip curled in a snarl as he pulled his car up and turned off the engine, in front of the Beach Café. Taking a glinting silver knife from the dashboard, Frankie LaSalle got out, slammed his car door shut, and hurried through the torrential rain to the side entrance of the isolated café.

Fifteen

"Where did the police say we were supposed to meet them?" Jessica was scowling with concentration as she squinted through the impenetrable rain at the slippery road before her. The weather was worsening by the minute. Mudslides made the highways treacherous, as gushing water streamed down from the mountains to the ocean. Debris littered the roads, and the black sky was brightened only by jagged flashes of lightning. Jessica gritted her teeth, struggling to keep the Fiat from going into a spin.

"Turn here," Maria instructed her. "They said they had a report of a little girl seen near a bridge between Route Nine and the Pacific Highway. They're meeting us at the next crosslight."

Jessica swore under her breath, pulling the

Fiat off onto the muddy shoulder just in front of a large tree that had been struck by lightning and now blocked the road. "We're going to have to go the rest of the way on foot," she told Maria, zipping her slicker up and jumping out of the car. "Let's try calling Taryn's name."

For the next few hundred yards, they stumbled along the shoulder of the road, clinging to each other for support. The storm was growing increasingly violent. The wind tore at them and churned up waves that looked big enough to swallow up the beach. Rain pelted the muddy cliffs bordering the highway, carving them with brown rivers that gushed down into the sea. Every time lightning flashed, Jessica jumped about a mile, nearly yanking Maria's arm from its socket. "Taryn!" she shouted until her throat was raw. "Taryn!"

"There's a squad car!" Maria shouted over the sound of the surf and rain. Jessica saw a red light flashing in the distance and quickened her pace. Maybe they had found Taryn!

"Oh, my Lord!" Maria screamed, her hands flying to her face. Jessica broke into a run, straining to see what had frightened Maria so badly.

Then she caught sight of Taryn. Her knees crumpled from fear.

A small footbridge near the cross lights had been snapped nearly in two by the tremendous power of the rising, surging river. All that remained were a few boards, a tiny platform suspended by the flimsy structure that still stood. Water continued to rush over the broken bridge; there was no telling how long the skeleton could stand.

And cowering on the jagged platform was Taryn, sobbing wildly, her suitcase clutched in her arms.

Jessica could barely breathe. It looked as though the entire bridge was about to collapse. Taryn would tumble down into the churning water beneath her and be killed!

"We don't know what to do," one of the policemen told Maria, putting an arm around her to steady her. "We're trying to get her to come toward us so we can reach her. But she won't move. She's too frightened."

Jessica stared in horror at the space separating the little platform from the solid ledge of land they were standing on. It wasn't very far, but as long as Taryn stayed at the far end, no one could grab her. How on earth were they going to get to her?

"If those boards were stable, we could try to jump to her. But we're afraid she'll fall," the second officer explained.

"Taryn! It's me, Maria!" Maria called. But Taryn was crying too hard to hear the words.

"There has to be some way," the first policeman shouted frantically. "That wooden support could give way any second. We've got to get to her!"

Jessica stared at the child with mounting terror. "Listen, she likes me," she said. "Maybe I can coax her into my arms. If you two hold onto me, do you think I could lean across to her?"

The officer frowned as he looked at the gap. "Well, if she'd come to the edge—"

"Let's try it," Jessica urged. "Grab hold of me and let me see if I can convince her to come to me."

Maria's face went white. "Jessica, are you sure you'll be all right?"

Suddenly a sharp crack echoed over the wind. A board had snapped off the platform. Taryn covered her face with her hands. They all heard her thin, pathetic scream.

"Come on. We can't waste any more time!" Jessica shrieked. The next minute she had ripped off her slicker so the policemen could grasp her by the waist. As they did, Jessica heard the sound of an ambulance's siren. She took a deep breath, trying not to look down at the swirling water beneath her. "Taryn!" she cried. The police strained outward with her, but even so, Jessica couldn't get anywhere near the petrified child. Taryn wouldn't budge, not even an inch. She just stared at Jessica, tears coursing down her cheeks.

"It's no good," Jessica called back to the policemen. "I can't get close enough."

"Can you get her to come toward you?" one of them asked.

Jessica's mind was a blank. Then suddenly she thought of something. "Taryn!" she cried again. "Come here, Taryn. I have a secret to tell you."

Taryn's eyes were now glued to Jessica. Jessica knew it wasn't her imagination. Taryn had stopped crying long enough to listen.

"Once there was a wicked little girl named Taryn," Jessica shouted, reaching out her arms. "She was so wicked she wouldn't come when Jessica called her. She just sat there and sat there. She was *so* wicked, and do you know what happened to her?"

Taryn stared at her, dumbounded.

"Come here, Taryn," Jessica called, stretching forward as far as she could. "Come here, and I'll tell you what happened to that wicked little girl."

The next thing she knew Taryn was creeping toward her, her blue eyes round with terror.

"Closer, Taryn!" Jessica cried, the words tearing her sore, hoarse throat. "Come closer, one little bit closer, and I'll tell you about that wicked little girl!" She felt the policemen gripping her waist with all their might. Just a little farther. . . . Jessica felt Taryn's fingers brush her own. She took a deep breath and grabbed the little girl by the wrists. Then, using all the strength she had, she pulled her off the platform.

Taryn screamed. At that second an enormous surge of muddy water struck the boards, sweeping them away. Jessica thought her lungs would burst; she could barely breathe she was holding on so tight. Then the policemen were pulling her back, and she and Taryn were both tumbling to the ground.

Taryn was saved.

Maria scooped Taryn up in her arms. Jessica hugged them both, then brushed the water and mud from Taryn's face. She had never seen anyone look so wet and woebegone. Taryn's hair was plastered to her head; her teeth chattered with cold and exhaustion; her whole body trembled violently. "She's been sick. She's got a bad fever," Maria told the ambulance attendants as they lifted Taryn from her arms.

"That was a very brave thing you did, young woman," the first policeman said to Jessica, putting out his hand to shake hers. "You saved her life."

Jessica could barely speak. She suddenly felt as weak as a kitten. More than anything, she just wanted to sit down and cry. "We have to call her parents." She forced the words out despite the tightness of her throat.

"Right. I'm going to get their names from you and then send you two on to the hospital with the amublance. We'll call the parents and direct them to you."

Jessica listened dumbly while Maria gave him the numbers of Mr. Bennet's club and Mrs. Bennet's mother's house. She still felt too dazed to believe what had just happened. She hoped Taryn would be all right.

"Want me to tell you more about the wicked little girl?" she asked the child in the back of the ambulance as they waited for the driver to get in and for Maria to finish talking to the police.

But Taryn didn't answer. Her eyes were tightly closed. She was breathing heavily, and her face was flushed.

Jessica felt incredibly frightened for her, in a different way than she had been when the child had been trapped out over the water. She wished they would all hurry—all of them!—and get Taryn to a hospital, where someone could finally take care of her.

"That must be Jessica." Josh looked up from his magazine.

"Want me to get it?" Lucy asked, cradling Sam in her arms.

"Nope. I've got it." Josh crossed the living room to the front hall and opened the door.

"Hi," a slender, dark-haired man said, stepping inside and looking around him with a distraught expression. "You're Josh Sargent, right?"

"Yes," Josh said, surprised. "Who are you?"

"I'm sorry. My name is Jody Philips. I'm Tony's manager. I didn't mean to be so abrupt and come charging in here this way. It's just that I have reason to believe Tony's in danger. Apparently Frankie LaSalle got this address out of Tony's secretary somehow, and we're afraid—"

"Lucy!" Josh called. He was still gripping the doorknob so hard his knuckles whitened. Lucy hurried into the front hall, Sam still in her arms. "Lucy, this man says he's Jody Philips. Is this the man you told that Tony's at the Beach Café?"

"N-n-no," Lucy stammered. "Omigosh," she shrieked, suddenly clutching the baby so tightly he squealed. Her face drained of all color as she realized what had happened. If the man who had come by wasn't Jody, then she had pointed Frankie LaSalle right in the direction of the Beach Café!

"Let's call the police." Jody tried to keep his movements controlled and calm, but his voice was shaking. "Where did you say he was? The Beach what?"

"The Beach Café," Lucy whispered, her face ashen.

They had rushed into the living room. Josh grabbed the phone.

"I can't believe this is happening," Josh said, his eyes wide with fear. He couldn't stand the thought of his cousin being in danger. "What can we do? There's got to be something—"

"We haven't got a second to lose," Jody said grimly. "Let's just hope we get there before it's too late."

"Where is she?" Audrey Bennet flew into the first-floor waiting room of the Lionel Whiting Hospital in downtown Malibu. "Where's my baby?"

"Mrs. Bennet!" Maria cried, jumping to her feet. "It was my fault," she sobbed brokenly. "If I hadn't been on the phone—"

"She's in there." Jessica pointed to a room down the hall. "But the doctors are making us wait out here."

Audrey looked terrible. Her hair was in disarray, and her makeup was streaky. Still, for all that Jessica couldn't help thinking that for the first time she looked *real*. The panic-stricken expression in her eyes made her seem like a human being, like someone who had real emotions.

"My poor little girl," Audrey moaned, her eyes filling with tears. "I've been such an idiot. It wasn't your fault, Maria. It was mine. Completely, totally my fault. If I had been there

157

today, this never would have happened. If I hadn't acted so selfishly . . . but I never had time for her. Never. I treated her like—like— Oh, it's all my fault!"

"No," a gruff voice said. Jessica looked up in surprise to see Malcolm Bennet standing in the doorway of the waiting room. "Not at all your fault," he added, crossing the room toward her. "What about me? Was I ever there for her, or for you? No. I was too busy with my club, with my stupid friends. I was too wrapped up in my own life to give either one of you what you needed. I've been no kind of father, Audrey. I've let that poor child down time after time."

"Oh, Mal," Audrey whispered.

"Mr. and Mrs. Bennet?" the doctor inquired, stepping into the room and consulting his clipboard. "We'd like you to come in now. Taryn is a very sick little girl. I'd better warn you, unless her fever breaks soon, we really can't make any promises about her recovery. We're doing what we can for her. She's been given ice baths in the hope of lowering her temperature."

Jessica grabbed Maria's arm.

"Please," Audrey gasped. "Let us see her!"

"She keeps asking for Jessica," the doctor said, looking around quizzically. "Anyone here by that name?"

"Here," Jessica said weakly.

"Why don't you come in with us?" Audrey

turned her tear-stained face beseechingly in Jessica's direction.

Jessica nodded speechlessly. "You come, too," she urged Maria in a hoarse whisper. One by one they filed into the room where Taryn tossed fitfully in the narrow bed, her face crimson and her eyes bright with fever.

Jessica was overcome with pity for the little girl. She just hoped there was something she could do this time to help—that she might be given another chance to save the child.

But for now, all she could do was sit by with the others, and watch and wait. The doctor said they could do nothing more until the fever broke.

"I should say. one thing," he said seriously, addressing all of them. "She needs to want to make it. I don't know how else to put it, but we see it again and again in cases like this. If any of you can think of some way to help give her the will to come through . . ."

No one said a word. They all looked hopelessly at one another, struggling to keep their emotions under control.

Through the window in Taryn's room Jessica could see the sky beginning to clear. The storm outside was almost over, she thought bitterly.

But the storm inside was only just beginning.

Sixteen

"Well, it looks like it's beginning to clear a little bit," Elizabeth said, letting out her breath as she stared out at the stormy sea.

Jamie was holding her hand tightly. "You've been scared to death, haven't you?"

Elizabeth nodded, flashing him an embarrassed smile. "I guess I have been. But I think we're out of the worst of it now."

For the last twenty minutes, she and Jamie had been watching the storm crash over the water, listening to the rain pound down on the roof of the café. By the time Elizabeth had arrived, it was too late to consider heading back home—the storm was too severe. They were stranded, along with two waiters and the restaurant's manager. None of them dared leave.

"I think we're all going to live!" declared one of the waiters triumphantly, setting down two glasses of iced tea with a flourish.

Elizabeth giggled and raised her glass to toast Jamie. The waiter retreated, and they had the cozy, storm-proof dining room all to themselves. She and Jamie resumed the very personal conversation they'd been having.

"I'm going to talk to my parents about you when they come up for the Fourth. But I have a feeling they won't approve of it. You're so much older than I am." Elizabeth fiddled shyly with her teaspoon.

Jamie looked pained. He cleared his throat, tightening his hand around hers. "Liz, what if I were to tell you . . ."

"Tell me what?" Elizabeth prompted. But Jamie never got a chance to respond. The door of the Beach Café burst open, and a big, swarthy man charged into the room. Something glittered in his hand, and Elizabeth froze with terror. It was a knife!

The man edged his way toward them, his dark eyes flashing with fury. "What have you done to yourself, Sargent?" he sneered, circling around their tiny table. A waiter, who had walked in from the kitchen, froze in alarm.

Jamie half-rose from the table, his face contorting with anger. "How did you find me?" he demanded.

"Jamie Galbraith," the man said tauntingly, making a threatening gesture with the knife. "You think you can get away with anything you please, don't you? Just because you're a big celebrity, you think you can mess around with my girlfriend as soon as I'm out of the picture! Well, I'll tell you something, Sargent. No one messes with Frankie LaSalle. You understand me? *No one.*"

Elizabeth's mouth was as dry as cotton. She couldn't have moved for the world. *What on earth is going on?* she wondered, dizzy with fear. *Why is this man threatening Jamie? Why is he calling him Sargent?*

"You're not going to get away with this, Frankie," Jamie was saying in a calm voice, backing slightly away from the table toward the glass wall of the café. "How did you find out where I was?" he repeated. Elizabeth knew Jamie well enough to read his intentions in his eyes. He was stalling for time. At least, she thought she knew him.

Frankie grimaced at Tony. "That little twit of a secretary you've got in L.A. gave it all away. I gave her a great line about being with the police, and she fell for it, hook, line, and sinker. She told me you were pretending to be Jamie Galbraith, college boy, hanging out at your cousin's place in Malibu."

Elizabeth felt a wild tremor run through her.

She could barely believe what she was hearing. Jamie wasn't Jamie at all. Then who was he? She pressed the palms of her hands to her temples as if she could force her mind to settle down, start working to find a way out of this nightmare. Because she knew one thing—whoever Jamie was, she loved him. And his life was in danger.

"Listen, Frankie. Nothing happened between Lisa and me. It's all a mistake. We just had one drink together, that's all. She was lonesome! If I'd known about you—"

"You stupid stars," Frank said savagely, lunging forward, a menacing look on his face. "You think just because you're famous you can take anything you want from anybody. Well, that just isn't the way it is, guy. I'm going to teach you a lesson once and for all!"

The next thing Elizabeth knew, Frankie had sprung at Jamie, the knife flashing in his hand. She screamed, jumping to her feet, knocking the chair over behind her. "Help us!" she hollered to the waiters. Frankie was on top of Jamie, pinning him down. The café was filled with the horrible sound of panting and physical contact as the two struggled on the floor.

With a sudden sharp wrench of his body, Jamie rolled out from under Frankie's grasp. They were on their feet again. "I'm gonna get you," Frankie kept grunting. Jamie swung at him, missed, and swore. Taking advantage of his loss of balance, Frankie grabbed Jamie by his collar, the knife gleaming in his right hand. Jamie screamed. Elizabeth felt a wave of dizziness as she saw a line of red blood across the shoulder of Jamie's pale yellow shirt.

"Get the knife!" one of the waiters was shouting at her. But Elizabeth didn't have time to think strategy. She acted purely on instinct. Grabbing the pewter vase from the center of the table, she struck Frankie as hard as she could on the back of his head. With a terrible groan he fell forward—right on top of Jamie—and the knife clattered to the floor.

In an instant the waiters were helping Elizabeth pull the man off Jamie. "Are you OK?" Elizabeth asked in a shaky voice. Her eyes began to flood with tears. Jamie's shoulder was bleeding steadily. If he was badly hurt . . .

"Everyone, freeze!" a harsh voice barked. "This is the police." Elizabeth spun around as the door slammed back and three policemen ran in, followed by a man in a gray suit.

"Tony! Are you all right?" The man hurried over to them.

Tony, Elizabeth thought, dazed. *Tony Sargent?* Suddenly she didn't know whether to laugh or cry. She felt worn out from everything that had happened, in no condition to piece together the fragments of the puzzle.

"Is this the guy?" The policeman lifted Frankie to his feet.

Tony sat up, holding a scrap of tablecloth to his shoulder. "Elizabeth knocked him out," he said admiringly, looking at her. "She saved my life!"

Jody turned to Elizabeth. "I'm Jody Philips, Tony's manager. Tony, you gave us a heck of a scare. Are you cut badly?"

Tony shook his head. "He nicked me with the knife, that's all."

"I think you're going to need stitches," the café manager observed, crouching down to examine his shoulder. "What about him?" He jerked his head at Frankie. "Is he all right?"

"Well, this young lady really gave it to him." One of the policemen grinned. "He's out, all right. And he'll have quite a headache when he comes around. Meanwhile, we're going to take him down to the station. Mr. Philips, do you think you can come with us and deal with the paperwork? That way your friend here can go straight to the hospital in one of our squad cars and get his shoulder fixed up."

"You have to take care of yourself, Mr. Sargent," the other policeman said with a shy smile. "We wouldn't want you hurt. Our daughters would never forgive us!"

Tony was staring at Elizabeth, his face pale. "If it's all right with you, Jody, I'd like to go right to the hospital—with Elizabeth. There are a few things I'd like to explain to her."

"Whatever you say," Jody said. Elizabeth was still too light-headed to fully register what was happening. Before she knew it, she found herself climbing into the back of a squad car with Jamie—*Tony*—who was still holding the tablecloth to his shoulder. Suddenly Elizabeth felt sick to her stomach. She bit her lip as tears sprang to her eyes.

"Look," Tony said, putting his free hand on her knee. "I have a lot of things to say to you, but the first thing is that I'm sorry I lied to you, Liz. I'm sorry I pretended to be someone I'm not."

Elizabeth didn't answer. A tear rolled down her cheek, and she looked away, staring out the window at the flooded streets as they drove down Breakwater Way.

"I mean it," Tony went on. "I came out to Malibu because I was in serious trouble. Frankie LaSalle has been after me for months. Do you realize you saved my life?"

Elizabeth turned back to him, her throat aching. "I really cared for you," she choked out. "I couldn't have done anything else."

"Cared? Past tense?" Tony looked at her, intensely, helplessly.

Elizabeth didn't answer. She couldn't find the words.

"Jody convinced me Malibu was the safest

place," he said softly. "I got professional makeup men. They dyed my hair brown and gave me contact lenses to make my eyes dark. The whole thing happened so fast. All of a sudden I was out here, and I had to be Jamie Galbraith to everyone."

"But did Josh and Lucy know?" Elizabeth was still confused.

Tony nodded. "Josh is my cousin. He was worried about me. He agreed with Jody that this was the best way to go."

"But what about me?" Elizabeth asked, her voice quavering. "Was I just something to keep you busy while you were stuck out here? Something to keep you from being bored until you could get back to your real life?"

She didn't mean to sound bitter, but she was starting to realize the enormity of what had occurred. She had fallen in love with Jamie Galbraith, but Jamie Galbraith didn't exist.

"That isn't what happened at all." Tony's eyes were warm and serious as they fixed on hers. "Liz, I want to say something now, and you can take it any way you want, OK? But just give me a chance. Just hear me out."

"All right," Elizabeth whispered.

"When I came out here, I thought it was going to be a drag. I hadn't seen Josh for a long time, and I wasn't big on the idea of hiding out for a few weeks—or longer. I admit it. But I didn't have a choice. What had happened was that I'd gotten involved, very briefly, with this—this groupie." His voice became bitter. "It turned out she was Frankie's girlfriend. The guy's wacko, Liz. He's been in prison, but I think they should institutionalize him after this. Anyway, I was scared. Really scared. He was making all these threatening calls, making me feel like my days were numbered."

"That's awful," Elizabeth said. She couldn't help feeling a rush of sympathy.

"Yeah. Well, I started thinking about a lot of things. Supposedly there's nothing like a glimpse of your own mortality to make you start evaluating, and reevaluating. Liz, you're probably going to think this sounds crazy, but I've always wanted to be Jamie Galbraith."

"What do you mean?" she asked uncertainly.

"Don't get me wrong. I don't mean I don't like being Tony Sargent. Most of the time it's great. But it's a strange life, Liz. I'm seventeen—only seventeen—and I've already had more than my share of certain kinds of experience. I've traveled all over the world, I've stayed in the best places, I've got more money than I could ever spend. I have my own apartment, my own secretary, my own manager. But—"

Elizabeth didn't take her eyes from his. "Go on," she said, her gentle voice warm with emotion.

"But there are other things I've never come near. There are other experiences I've never had—and maybe never would have had at all if it weren't for Jamie Galbraith. And for you."

"I still don't get it," Elizabeth said slowly. She wanted to understand so badly, but she felt incredibly stupid. When she thought of all the idiotic things she'd said to him, to Tony Sargent, who was such a huge star . . .

"I've always wanted a chance just to be myself," Tony said feelingly. "You know, to be able to say things and hear *real* reactions. To meet a girl and tell her I thought she was beautiful—and see how she reacted to *me*, not to Tony Sargent. Does that make sense?"

"Yes," Elizabeth said softly, "I guess it does."

She couldn't help but wonder what was going to happen to the magical thing she and Jamie had shared. It looked as though their brand-new love was a thing of the past now. Elizabeth felt as if her heart were breaking. Whatever he said to her, however nice he tried to be, she knew it had to be over. How could he ever really care for her—for quiet, serious Elizabeth Wakefield?

"Here we are, folks," the policeman said, opening the soundproof shield that separated the front seat from the back. "The Lionel Whiting Hospital. If you head into the emergency room, I think someone should be able to stitch that cut up right away."

"Thank you very much, officer." Tony got out and opened the door for Elizabeth.

"One favor." The policeman looked sheepish. "I don't suppose I could get your autograph? My little girl would never forgive me if I let you get away without it."

Elizabeth shivered. A light rain was still falling. She watched Tony scribble on a slip of paper, then hand it through the window of the squad car. She couldn't believe any of this had really happened.

"Sorry about that." Tony put his arm around her shoulder. "Liz—"

"I just want to know one thing," Elizabeth said abruptly. "Where is any of this going to leave *us*? You can't be Jamie Galbraith anymore. Does that mean—?"

"I don't know what it means," Tony said uncertainly, looking away from her. "We've both been through a lot today, Liz. Maybe we should wait until things have calmed down a little to figure out where we stand."

Elizabeth's eyes stung with tears. She should have guessed as much. Now that he was safe, he would forget all about her. He had kept himself busy while he was stuck in Malibu by seeing her, but that was it.

"Hey!" Tony peered ahead of them through

the rain, his hand closing tightly on her shoulder. "Isn't that Jessica?"

Elizabeth stared. Sure enough, Jessica was walking out the main entrance of the hospital!

Seventeen

"I can't believe it." Jessica's eyes were as wide as saucers, and her mouth dropped open. "You mean that guy, Jamie Galbraith, is really *Tony Sargent*?"

Elizabeth nodded dumbly.

"Omigosh!" Jessica shrieked, clapping her hand to her forehead. "I've been living under the same roof as Tony Sargent for *days*, and I never even knew it? What an idiot I am!" She moaned. "And I thought he was such a complete creep. I've been treating him horribly. He must think I'm such a *jerk*."

The twins were standing outside the emergency room, waiting for Tony while doctors attended to the cut on his shoulder. In their initial excitement, the two stories had been so jumbled it was hard for either to figure out what had happened to the other. Elizabeth was beside herself when she heard about Taryn. She couldn't help being so worried that she almost forgot about the mess with Tony. Almost.

"But what were you doing with Jamie—I mean Tony—at this deserted restaurant on the beach in the first place?" Jessica demanded.

Elizabeth reddened. "Uh—"

"Elizabeth Wakefield!" Jessica squealed and grabbed her arm. "Do you mean to tell me that you've been seeing Tony Sargent? *Tony Sargent?*"

"I didn't know he was Tony," Elizabeth said with a sigh.

"Well, you don't look very happy about it," Jessica remarked. "Boy, if *I* were lucky enough to. . . . I'm *such* an idiot," she added tragically. "Here I was, all ready to meet Tony, and when a 'friend of the family' moved in, I didn't even stop to think it could be him!"

"You mean you knew Tony was related to the Sargents? How come you never told me?"

Jessica blinked. "Well—I didn't think you'd care. You didn't even know who he was until a month ago."

Elizabeth shook her head. "Let's go upstairs and see Taryn. Honestly, Jess, I just want to forget the whole thing with Tony."

"You can't forget it," Jessica objected. "Here

the poor guy is, practically bleeding to death in the emergency room. The very least you could do is convince him to come up and see Taryn. I bet a visit from a big star will do wonders for her." Her eyes twinkled.

Elizabeth smirked. "I don't suppose the visit from the big star is of any interest to *you*, is it?"

Jessica was all innocence. "Don't be such a stick in the mud, Liz. Who spent the whole day sliding around in the storm, rescuing Taryn, while you were off gallivanting with celebrities?"

Elizabeth sighed. "OK, I'll ask him to come up when they're finished with him." She could tell when she was licked.

Several minutes later she reported, "He'll join us when they're through. He needs seven stitches. Come on, Jess. I'm not going to feel better till I've seen Taryn."

Elizabeth didn't know what was making her feel worse—guilt over leaving Taryn alone and concern for her health, or disappointment and frustration about Tony Sargent.

But she did know one thing. The perfect summer Jessica had promised her had turned pretty rapidly into a major disaster!

"I don't think she looks any better." Audrey Bennet sighed, pushing her dark hair back from her forehead. "She just can't break that high fever!"

Elizabeth leaned over the little hospital bed, her eyes anxious. Poor Taryn, she thought sadly. She was so obviously uncomfortable. She breathed with great difficulty, apparently from the congestion in her chest, and her face was blotched with fever. Her blue eyes were bright, but they didn't seem to be focusing very clearly on anything. "Hi, Taryn," Elizabeth said, leaning closer with a smile.

"Jessica?" Taryn said with difficulty.

"Jess, she wants you," Elizabeth whispered, disappointed.

Audrey was crying softly. "I keep feeling there has to be something I can do to get through to her. I know it sounds stupid, but I feel like— well, I feel like she needs to know her father and I are behind her. The doctors seem to think she's given up!"

Jessica was thoughtful for a minute. "I wonder . . ." she said finally, joining Audrey and putting a hand gently on her arm. "Listen, I've been playing a game with Taryn all summer, which she really seems to respond to." She outlined the silly "secrets" she'd been telling Taryn. "*My* father used to tell stories like that to Liz and me when we were young. And we really loved them. Why don't you try telling her a wicked little girl story, and see what happens?"

Audrey looked doubtful. "Do you really think it'll work?"

"It couldn't hurt," Jessica said with a smile.

"OK," Audrey agreed, squeezing her hand. "Thanks, Jess!"

She crossed the room to Taryn's bed, a desperate, determined smile on her beautiful face. "Taryn," she murmured, laying a cool hand on the child's forehead. Her daughter's eyes fixed on her, dully and without recognition.

"It's me. It's Momma," Audrey whispered.

The whole room was quiet.

"Taryn," Audrey whispered again, "want me to tell you a secret?"

Taryn's eyes filled with tears. A minute later she nodded her head, gazing at her mother.

"Once there was a little girl named Taryn," her mother said gently. "She was a very beautiful little girl, and very, very good. Only she had one problem. She had a wicked mommy and daddy. They didn't mean to be wicked, because above all else they adored Taryn and they knew how good she was. But they were wicked to each other, and sometimes they were wicked to their little girl, too."

The tension in the room mounted rapidly. Jessica and Elizabeth were mesmerized. "Should I keep telling the story?" Audrey asked Taryn in a quiet voice.

Taryn nodded again. A tear spilled from her

eye and ran down her cheek. Elizabeth felt her throat ache with tears.

"Well, Taryn's mommy and daddy love her very much. And they love each other, too. They want to try to make a new beginning, only they need their little girl to get better quick and stop feeling so sick."

"Momma," Taryn croaked, putting her little arms up.

The next minute Audrey was scooping her daughter up in her arms, laughing and crying at the same time. "Oh, Taryn," she sobbed, stroking the child's hair with her hand. "My poor little Taryn."

"Hey, let me in on this!" Malcolm Bennet exclaimed hoarsely. The twins had nearly forgotten his presence. Now he crossed the room from where he had been standing in the corner and threw his arms around his wife and daughter.

Elizabeth and Jessica hugged each other, their eyes mirroring the emotions they were feeling—relief, sympathy, and joy. Elizabeth was sure that Taryn was going to pull through and that things were going to be considerably different around the Bennet household from now on.

The place she had left that afternoon was a house; the place she would be returning to would be a *home*.

*　　*　　*

The Bennets dropped Tony, Elizabeth, and Jessica off at the Beach Café, where they all got into the Camaro. Elizabeth drove Jessica and Tony to the intersection where Jessica had left the Fiat earlier that day. "I still can't believe Frankie's finally in custody," Tony said. "I've got to admit I'm relieved."

"What now?" Jessica asked brightly. "Are you going back to L.A.?"

Elizabeth sighed as she drove. She had a feeling that whatever Tony's plans were, they didn't include her.

"Well, actually, no. I didn't know whether or not I'd be able to do it, but Jody has lined up a big concert for me at the rock festival in Oakwood Park next Saturday. The proceeds all go to charity, for research into children's cancer. We were afraid I'd still be in disguise, but now it looks like I can stick around for it." He was quiet for a minute. Then he turned to Elizabeth. "Needless to say, I hope you both come. Jody has a bunch of free passes for you if you're interested."

"Of course we're interested!" Jessica squealed.

Elizabeth knew Tony was looking quizzically at her, but she kept her eyes on the road. "Well, here we are," she said, pulling up behind the little red Fiat.

"I really would like it if you'd come." Tony put a hand on her shoulder. His eyes didn't leave her face.

Elizabeth cleared her throat. "The concert sounds very nice," she said flatly.

"Well . . ." Tony looked disappointed. "I guess I have to change back to my old self." He forced himself to sound brighter as he looked down at his wrinkled khakis. He pushed back his fake glasses self-consciously. "I guess next time you see me I'll look pretty different."

"Where will you go now?" Jessica asked. "You're not going to still stay at the Sargents', are you?"

Tony shook his head. "No. I'm moving in with Jody at the Malibu Inn for the rest of the week. After the concert I'll probably head back to L.A."

Elizabeth swallowed. "I'd better get going," she said, her voice dull. "I think the Bennets probably want me to get the car back."

Tony flushed. Jessica saw his jaw clench tightly. "I guess I'll see you around," he said, a question in his voice. "Liz, can I call you?"

Elizabeth looked at him. She wished she knew what he was thinking.

But she did, she reminded herself. It was one thing that afternoon, when he was still Jamie Galbraith and needed someone to hang around with, someone to help him pass the time.

Now everything was back to "normal." Tony had returned to his own world, and a barrier had gone up between them. He was a huge star, and who was she? Just an ordinary girl.

Jamie Galbraith had been a dream come true. But the dream was over now. By the time Tony had packed his bag and settled in at the Malibu Inn, she thought, he would have forgotten she even existed.

"I really don't see what good it would do for us to try to see each other again," Elizabeth said stiffly.

Tony's painfully silent acceptance of her words tore at her heart. She wished there was some way—but it was impossible. There was no point in getting her hopes up. They would only be dashed sooner or later.

No, it was best this way. If only it didn't hurt so much to watch him walk away.

Eighteen

"I really mean it, Jess," Elizabeth said, lying back on her towel and putting the straps of her jade-green one-piece off her shoulders. "If you still want to switch jobs, I'm willing. After what you did for Taryn . . ."

"It was nothing," Jessica said nonchalantly. She tossed her hair back and looked contentedly around her. The twins were at the public beach behind the Bennets', soaking up the sun while Lila and Ben bobbed about in the waves on plastic floats.

"It wasn't just saving her life, either," Elizabeth continued. A shadow crossed her face as she remembered the events that had taken place earlier that week. It was Monday now, and Taryn was home from the hospital, recovering quickly from the combination of flu and bronchi-

183

tis. "I don't know how you did it, but you really helped Audrey get through to her."

"Are things really better between them, then?" Jessica asked with interest as she squeezed a generous amount of suntan lotion onto one arm.

Elizabeth was thoughtful. "Well, things can't become perfect overnight. There's still a long way to go. But at least they're trying now. Malcolm and Audrey have been home all this time. They really seem to be getting along, and they're just drowning Taryn in love and affection."

"Well, that wasn't my doing," Jessica said.

"But you were the one who got through to Taryn first," Elizabeth insisted. "That's why I think we should talk to the Bennets and the Sargents about changing jobs for the rest of the summer, if you still want to, that is."

Jessica was quiet for a minute, then she shrugged casually. "To tell you the truth, I don't see any reason to change now, Liz. We might as well just stay put. I've gotten kind of used to little Sam's room!"

Jessica didn't see any reason to add that she and Cliff had had a long talk about this very issue that same day. Cliff had made his feelings clear. He loved spending time with Jessica, but he thought their romance would suffer if she were to live right next door. It wouldn't seem as special. She had tried hard to change his mind, but he'd finally convinced her that switching jobs just wasn't worth it.

At the same time there was no point in lessening her twin's opinion of her, Jessica thought, especially now that Elizabeth clearly considered her a candidate for Woman of the Year. Better to keep quiet about why she was content to stay at the Sargents'!

Elizabeth was secretly relieved. Even though Tony had moved out of the Sargents' house, the place was still haunted for her. The thought of *living* there—of sitting day after day in the living room where they had talked for the first time . . . Elizabeth squeezed her eyes shut against the picture of Jamie Galbraith—Tony Sargent—standing on the front steps, a tentative smile on his lips.

"Lila and Ben look so cute together," Jessica observed with a giggle. "I think he's converted her once and for all from her ideas about older men."

"It sure looks that way," Elizabeth said absently. "Where's Cliff, by the way?"

"He'll be here any minute." Jessica rolled over onto her stomach to look at her sister's watch. A frown crossed her face as she caught sight of Elizabeth's expression. "I feel kind of bad," she said suddenly. "I mean, Lila's got Ben, and I have Cliff. It doesn't seem fair that Tony had to go and ruin everything by taking Jamie Galbraith away with him!''

Elizabeth tried to look and sound as if she didn't care. "What difference does it make? It had to happen sooner or later."

Jessica looked wistful. "But it must have been so romantic, stealing away and meeting him secretly. I can't help being mad at Tony, on your behalf of course. Has he called?"

Elizabeth bit her lip. Jessica probably didn't realize how insensitive she was being. She couldn't know how low Elizabeth was feeling about everything these days. "Yes, he's called, but I haven't talked to him," she said.

Jessica was amazed. "Why not?"

"What's the use? It's over between us. The sooner I realize that, the better." Elizabeth gave her twin a look that clearly signaled the case was closed. But she couldn't close the case in her own thoughts as easily.

The night of the storm she'd gone home to the Bennets' in a state of confusion. She promised herself a good night's sleep would help, but when she got back, the Bennets wanted to talk. Audrey especially wanted Elizabeth's opinion on how they could best go about getting to know their little girl. They talked for hours, and the sun was coming up by the time Elizabeth went to bed, exhausted.

The next few days passed in a blur. There were

frequent visits to the hospital and tremendous relief as it became evident Taryn was getting better. Finally they were celebrating her coming home. The rest of Elizabeth's time was filled by seeing as much of Jessica and Lila as possible.

But, as Jessica had pointed out, perhaps with more truth than tact, their company was on one hand a much-needed distraction and on the other a constant reminder of Tony. Watching Lila and Ben together right now, for instance. It was so obvious that they were falling in love. The way Ben touched Lila's hand, the way Lila's face lit up when he whispered something in her ear . . .

Elizabeth's heart ached. Even the warmth of the sun, usually so therapeutic, didn't make her feel any better. If only she and Tony could have had a chance, a real chance, to get to know each other. She turned away from Jessica, hiding the tears that spilled from her eyes. She was remembering the incredible moment when Tony kissed her outside the restaurant in Santa Monica. She could almost relive the moment right now. The ocean was pounding behind them, and he took her in his arms, tracing the outline of her lips with his index finger. "Whatever happens, remember this," he had murmured then, leaning forward and kissing her deeply. . . .

Elizabeth found herself blushing as she remembered the way that kiss had affected her. Darn, she thought angrily. Why had this happened to her? Why had she fallen in love with someone who didn't even really exist?

"If it isn't my favorite twins!" Cliff Sherman called, striding toward them across the sand. He dropped his beach towel next to Jessica's. "I've missed you, Jess," he declared, planting a kiss on the top of her head.

"Mmm, me too," Jessica said huskily.

Then she shot a look at her twin and prodded Cliff with her elbow. "Did you ask him?" she hissed in a stage whisper.

"Oh, that's right," Cliff hissed back at her. "Hey, Liz," he said casually, "did I ever mention my friend Brent to you? He's a really nice guy. He goes to school with me, and he wants to be a writer, too. He and I and some of my other friends were thinking about going out for a pizza, and we were wondering if you wanted to come along with us."

Elizabeth shook her head. "That's really sweet of you both, but I really don't feel like doing much of anything today."

Jessica gave Cliff a desperate look. "Let's take a walk," she said impulsively, jumping to her feet and grabbing him by the hand.

"We'll be back soon," Cliff said to Elizabeth, who was flipping listlessly through the pages of her novel.

"Sure," Elizabeth said dully. She barely even noticed when they walked away.

As soon as they were safely out of earshot, Jessica pounded Cliff lightly on the shoulder. "It's so unfair. The whole thing is just too tragic for words." She sighed. "But I can't understand why she won't talk to him. She's not even giving him a chance. He *could* be madly in love with her. Cliff, what are we going to do?"

"Well," Cliff said thoughtfully, slinging his arm casually across Jessica's shoulder, "I'm not sure how much we really can do, Jess. The truth is your sister's probably right. The chance of anything really working out between her and Tony Sargent isn't too great. They lead such different kinds of lives. Maybe she's just doing all she can to make the pain she's feeling come fast, so she can face it and get over it."

"What do you mean?" Jessica's wide eyes were puzzled.

"Well, maybe she feels that seeing Tony again, or even talking on the phone, would be too hard for her right now. I think we should give her the benefit of the doubt and trust her judgment about all this."

"I don't know." Jessica shook her head. "I think Liz is denying her feelings. I think she needs to see him again—at least once."

Cliff shrugged, then leaned his head down to nuzzle Jessica's neck. "Maybe you're right. I have to admit I'm kind of worried about Elizabeth, too. She really does seem down. Do you think it'd help her to go to Tony's concert tomorrow night?"

"I keep bringing it up, but she says she wouldn't go for anything." Jessica giggled. "You're tickling me!"

Cliff grinned and then was serious again. "Well, I think she should go. I think we should just drag her there. It might be hard seeing Tony, but maybe you're right. Maybe it's better for her to confront the situation instead of staying home and moping about it."

"OK," Jessica said, her sparkling eyes determined. "Only *you* have to convince her. I've already tried every way I know how. And you know how persuasive I can be."

"Do I ever!" Cliff smiled broadly, twisting a lock of Jessica's bright hair around his finger. "You're on. She'll be there."

Elizabeth was letting herself be lulled into a half-sleep by the sound of the waves. It was later that afternoon, and she was alone on the beach. Jessica and Cliff had gone back over to the Sargents', and Lila and Ben were renting a sailboat for the afternoon at the yacht club.

Elizabeth was oblivious to the feel of the sunlight on her skin. It was funny. All morning she had longed to be alone so she could think about

Tony in peace. Now she *was* alone, and she was miserable. Thinking only made her sad.

She didn't exactly know what upset her most about the whole thing with Tony. It had been such a long time since she had let herself feel so strongly about a guy, and at first it had seemed so wonderful, so worth the wait. But now she felt as though she'd been slapped in the face. The very worst was the fear that Tony had been using her, that she'd only imagined that he returned her feelings. She couldn't *know* that he had ever cared for her, even the slightest bit.

True, he'd said he did. But then as Jamie Galbraith, he'd said a lot of things that weren't true. Even the fact that he had called her three times from the Malibu Inn didn't have to mean anything.

Realistically Elizabeth knew that she and Tony Sargent could never stay involved with each other. He lived in a world she could barely even imagine, a world she suspected she wouldn't really like or approve of. Still, that didn't change her feelings. She wanted only to believe that he had cared, that she'd made some kind of impact on him. She couldn't bear it if while her heart was breaking, he might not even remember her name.

"Liz?" A small voice interrupted her introspection.

Elizabeth sat up with a start. "Taryn!" she

cried, putting her arms out as the little girl came shyly toward her. "What are you doing out of bed?"

"Momma said it was OK." Taryn put her thumb in her mouth and gave Elizabeth a crooked little smile. The next minute she was in Elizabeth's arms, her tousled head buried in her shoulder.

"Oh, Taryn," Elizabeth said, half happy and half sad. She rocked the little girl back and forth. Tears welled in her eyes, and at last she could hold back no longer. They came coursing down her cheeks, faster and faster.

"Why are you crying?" Taryn asked, reaching up to touch her wet face.

Elizabeth shook her head. She couldn't answer.

"Are you afraid no one loves you?" Taryn looked serious. "Because my mom says that people really do love each other. They just get confused sometimes and forget how to let each other know."

Elizabeth took a deep breath and pulled Taryn close, hugging her so hard she gasped.

"Your mother's right," Elizabeth said, fighting to control her runaway emotions.

She just wished she really believed that. Or that there was some way she could be sure.

Nineteen

"Aren't you glad now that you came? Aren't you lucky Cliff is so convincing?" Jessica asked, looking around at the crowded pavilion with an expression of rapture on her face. "I would've hated it if you hadn't been here tonight, Liz."

Elizabeth's face was pale despite her tan. "I guess I'm glad," she said faintly, watching the crowds with amazement. All of these people had come here to see Tony! It made her feel kind of dizzy. She couldn't believe just a short time ago they had been sitting alone together in the Beach Café, holding hands.

Lila nudged Jessica. "Look, there's the warm-up band, the Number One!"

Elizabeth and Jessica both recognized the

popular L.A. area band that Lila had booked for one of her big parties back in Sweet Valley.

"Let's find our seats," Ben said, studying one of the free passes Jessica had picked up that morning at the front desk of the Malibu Inn. Elizabeth had refused to accompany her, despite Jessica's insistence that she and Tony would probably bump into each other in the lobby and fall in love all over again.

"It's bad enough that you and Cliff are dragging me to his concert," Elizabeth had grumbled. "If you want to go so badly, then *you* go and pick up the tickets."

Unfortunately, Jessica hadn't seen Tony *or* Jody. The passes were in an envelope, but no note was enclosed.

"He got us incredible seats," Jessica pointed out. Elizabeth didn't respond. She had the same dull look on her face that came over her whenever Tony Sargent's name was mentioned. It made Jessica feel sad—sad and worried at the same time.

"Hey, this is incredible!" Ben exclaimed as they walked toward the front of the crowded pavilion. "We're practically in the front row!"

"What did you expect?" Jessica asked airily. She felt as though she were practically a star herself, attending Tony Sargent's concert at *his* request, the tickets a gift from the singer himself.

This was exactly why she'd come to Malibu. It was fantastic!

Finally the five were settled in their seats, right of center but only three rows from the front. They were in perfect view of the floodlit stage.

The warm-up band was setting up their equipment. The excitement mounted as throngs of people filled the pavilion.

Then all at once the lights dimmed, and the Number One came running onstage. The audience burst into applause.

Elizabeth leaned back in her seat, wishing she had stayed at home. Not that she didn't love rock concerts. It was just that she knew it was going to be incredibly painful seeing Tony up there in front of her, so near but still out of reach. Her stomach was tied in knots at the prospect. What would he look like, anyway, out of his disguise? She wondered if she would still feel something, looking at the "real" Tony Sargent. Maybe she had only been in love with the character he'd invented.

She had agreed to come along only because she wanted to shake herself out of the depression she was sinking into. Cliff was right. It was time to get her usual enthusiasm and cheerfulness back in gear. So here she was, listening to the pulse of the music, watching the people around her jump to their feet, clapping their hands and swaying, and she just wanted it to be over. She stared dumbly ahead of her, her eyes filled with tears.

The Number One finished their last song to tremendous applause. The butterflies in her stomach got considerably worse. Tony was next.

"That was the Number One!" the emcee shouted. Someone behind her whistled loudly, and Elizabeth felt the back of her neck prickle. "And now . . . the man you've all been waiting for! I won't keep him from you any longer—Tony Sargent!"

The crowd went wild. People jumped up and down screaming; confetti and streamers clouded the air. Elizabeth held her breath. Suddenly there he was! He looked fantastic. Her heart pounded as he ran to the front of the stage, picked up the mike, and faced the audience. "Hello, Malibu," he said with a wide, sexy smile. The sound of that familiar voice made tears leap into Elizabeth's eyes.

He looked like another person entirely. His hair was blond again and stood up a little in the front. He was wearing tight-fitting black jeans and a wrinkled white shirt unbuttoned halfway. But his voice—that incredible, husky voice. If she closed her eyes she could almost imagine they were alone together at the café, alone with the surf and the sand and the sun.

Tony put his hand up, waiting for the screams and whistles to die down. "I have a special song I want to start out with tonight," he said, his voice sending shivers up and down Elizabeth's spine. "A special song for a special girl. I wrote it this week, and my manager tells me we're going to make this one a hit single."

More applause followed this announcement, and again Tony waited for silence. "This song is called 'Summer Girl,' " he said, walking from one end of the stage to the other. "I just want to say that if Liz is anywhere out there tonight, this song is for you."

Elizabeth froze.

"Liz, that's you!" Jessica squealed excitedly, hitting her on the arm.

Elizabeth felt as if the wind had been knocked out of her. The lights were dimming further. One by one people held up lighters, candles, or matches, the little flames shining like thousands of tiny stars. She felt her own eyes light up with rekindled emotion.

Tony's voice was rich and throaty, and a sigh seemed to run around the pavilion as he began the song.

Summer girl, just one brief look,
One stolen moment, that was all it took.
All my life I'd waited for
A girl who was special, a girl who was more.

We really didn't have very long,

Time for a kiss, time for a song.
But summer girl, I think I always knew
My whole life, that it was you.

Wherever I go in this big cold world,
I'll be thinking of you, my summer girl,
Thinking of your smile and wondering when
My summer girl, we'll meet again.

We'll meet again,
I think I always knew,
My summer girl, that it was you.

Elizabeth tried to blink the tears out of her eyes, but it was impossible. She could hear the crowd going wild around her, but she felt as if she were set apart from them, removed in a tiny island of pain and emotion. She could feel Tony's eyes on hers as he finished the song, and suddenly she broke down, crying as if she'd never stop.

So he had cared for her after all! Suddenly Elizabeth was convinced that Tony Sargent was the most wonderful, awful thing that had ever happened to her in her entire life. She knew she would never see him again—that there was no way she could go backstage after the concert was over. What they had shared was too precious for that. It had existed only as long as the fiction of

Jamie Galbraith had existed, and now it was lost forever.

But she would never forget him. And she knew, listening to the heartbreaking swell of his voice as the song came to an end, that he would never forget her, either. She had been his summer girl. And he had reminded her what it was like to fall in love again, a love that was the most magical and poignant she had ever known.

BANTAM
SHOP-AT-HOME
C·A·T·A·L·O·G

Special Offer
Buy a Bantam Book
for only 50¢.

Now you can order the exciting books you've been wanting to read straight from Bantam's latest listing of hundreds of titles. *And* this special offer gives you the opportunity to purchase a Bantam book for only 50¢. Here's how:

By ordering any five books at the regular price per order, you can also choose any other single book listed (up to $4.95 value) for only 50¢. Some restrictions do apply, so for further details send for Bantam's listing of titles today.

Just send us your name and address and we'll send you Bantam Book's SHOP AT HOME CATALOG!

A LOVE TRILOGY
First there is <u>LOVING</u>.

Meet Caitlin, gorgeous, rich charming and wild. And anything Caitlin wants she's used to getting. So when she decides that she wants handsome Jed Michaels, there's bound to be some trouble. ☐ 24716/$2.95

Then there is <u>LOVE LOST</u>.

The end of term has arrived and it looks like the summer will be a paradise. But tragedy strikes and Caitlin's world turns upside down. Will Caitlin speak up and risk sacrificing the most important thing in her life?
☐ 25130/$2.95

And at last, <u>TRUE LOVE</u>.

Things are just not going the way Caitlin had planned, and she can't seem to change them! Will it take a disaster and a near-fatality for people to see the light? ☐ 25295/$2.95

Prices and availability subject to change without notice.

Buy them at your local bookstore or use this handy coupon for ordering: